Dedica

CW01507786

This is dedicated to the many people who supported me with patience as I rediscovered my love for Max and Rick after a difficult time. (Seriously, did any of us have a good 2020?) So, Amanda, Michael, Bethany, India, Angel, Sarah, Jeanette, Anka, Beth, Carolyn, Emma, and SJ made this story possible. Hell, Jeanette is better at keeping track of my characters' names than I am. Thank you to my whole cheering section for your encouragement, your emotional support, and your ability to stop my stupidity before I published it for everyone to see.

Chapter One

S pace was more boring than Max had anticipated. Even alien
kidnappings failed to live up to the drama movies had promised
him. He glared at the list of engine words the translator displayed and
wondered if Rick was still busy with his work. Tentacle sex was the one
part of space travel that did live up to the hype, but Max didn't want to
distract his partner. Maybe he could watch television with the kids.
They needed someone to remind them that the signals Rick was
picking up from space were fictional. Sometimes the kids assumed
human television was like the instructional videos about their home
planet.

However, if he spent all his time with the kids, their translation
problems would never get better. So he had to be an adult. He hated
adulting.

Hours later, Max was still fighting with a translation when the
door opened behind him. The slide of tentacles across decking was
slow enough that it could only be Rick. The children's smaller tentacles
made a more *sweep-sweep* sound. They were growing at a terrifying rate,
but they didn't have their father's bulk. Max paused the program as a
tentacle slid over his shoulder and Rick leaned into him. He was such a
cuddler.

As Max stroked the soft skin, Rick curled his limb around Max's
arm and used the fingers along the underside to tickle Max's wrist.
"Query," Rick asked, "am I husband?"

Max whipped his head about, and his brain stalled for a moment,
long enough for Rick's tentacles to twitch. "Answer. I see you as my

EARTH HUSBANDS ARE ODD
Lyn Gala

Warning

Table of Contents

husband," Max said before Rick could get his tentacles in a knot. No one could do guilt like Rick when his tentacles went all curly fries.

"Your answer appears partial," Rick said. Ever since he'd sent a snooper satellite to pick up Earth transmissions, Rick's ability to understand English had grown by leaps and bounds. Sometimes that was a boon. Sometimes Max missed the days when he could hide his feelings more easily.

After ending the computer program, Max turned in his chair. "I see you as my husband, but husband and marriage require making vows in front of witnesses and informing others of the intent to pair bond. Others did not see our vows." Max loved Rick, but sometimes he didn't feel married.

Rick made a quarter turn and studied Max with a new set of eyes. "Query. Others must be human to witness?"

"We are not going to Earth." Max could not handle the legal or emotional damage a trip to earth would inflict. To say he was disappointed with his home planet was an understatement. While part of him felt as if he should go home to defend his family and country, he already had a ship and family who needed protection. As much as he adored Rick, the damn octopus had the common sense of Urkel. When he'd found out Rick had turned off the proximity alarms because they were annoying, Max could practically hear "Did I do that?" in whale song.

Rick pulled tentacles closer to his body as he slid nearer. "Agreed. Human illogic is distressing. Moron is not required in definition of human, but many humans morons. I am grateful you are not moron."

That was an understatement. "I wish other humans would be less moronic."

The tentacles on the near side twitched. "Query. Witnesses others must be human?"

"You lost a conjunction there, buddy."

Rick pressed a tentacle against Max's stomach, and then he used the finger tentacles along the underside to tickle a vulnerable spot. Max's giggle ended in a snort so loud it made his nose sting. Max never should have taught the kids about the tickle monster. He pushed Rick away. Unfortunately, Rick had way more appendages than Max. So every time Max shoved one tentacle away, three more attacked him. Max ended up laughing so hard that he fell off the chair, and Rick caught him. Their limbs tangled, and Rick ended up sitting on Max's chest and shoulder before he stopped.

Max gasped for air and grinned like an idiot. "Bully," he whispered.

Rick blew a raspberry against Max's shoulder. After a minute, Rick said, "Query."

Max let his head *thunk* back against the floor. "Yes. I know. Can witnesses other than humans witness a marriage? I don't have a simple answer. Different human groups define marriage differently." Max did not want to discuss religion or gay marriage or various religions' views of gay marriage. He wondered if crazy radicals would be more or less offended by alien marriage. Whatever. Max didn't want to discuss this issue with non-humans. He'd had enough trouble trying to explain looting and planetary war. Apparently, most planets in this part of the universe reserved war for trying to kill individuals from other planets, not their own.

Human transmissions were making Max's life difficult. He hated having to explain these concepts to the children, especially Xander who never accepted a quick or easy answer.

"Query. How does Max define marriage?"

Max held up his hand, and Rick curled his tentacles around the fingers. "I define us as married. I like having sameness with you forever."

Several of Rick's tentacles waved before they curled around Max's arm. They lay on the floor, entwined. Max couldn't imagine ever being married to anyone else in the universe. When Rick got too heavy, Max started shifting. That made Rick pull back. "We retreat from space contiguous to Earth transmissions."

That was new. Up until this point, Rick had insisted that he needed seclusion to work on his computer program and the part of the galaxy close to Earth was exceptionally private. Max propped himself up on his elbow. "Why?"

Rick shifted down to Max's lap and his tentacles stilled. "I require trade for compensation."

"Okay," Max said slowly, not sure what Rick wasn't saying. "Query. Are we going back to the port where you hired me?" With access to the manufacturing machines in the upper decks, he had managed to produce clothing and some lightweight armor patterned off the equipment Rick had scavenged from the pirates. That, plus the weapons, made Max feel a little better about visiting a trading port.

Three tentacles curled. "The people are disliking the people."

Max snorted. "That made no sense." He scooted around so he could sit up, and Rick lifted himself a few inches so they were at eye level. "Now that you have more words, you have to be able to give me the names of different species."

Several of Rick's longer tentacles curled around Max's waist. Max was tempted to call Rick his cuddle bunny, and it felt nice to be able to touch without worrying about dirty looks or commanding officers. "People call themselves people." The translator's voice was equally unhelpful, but Max recognized Rick's belching version of "human" in his own voice.

"That's a problem. Give me a second." Max extricated himself from the tentacle nest.

"Query. Define problem." Rick followed Max to the computer and leaned against Max's back while he pulled up the translation program. Max had gotten terrifyingly good at working the glitchy thing.

"Answer. Human should not translate. Human should be human, not people."

"Query. Does not people mean people?" Again, Rick's voice belched out an approximation of the word "human."

"People only means a generic group."

"Query. How does one define human?"

That made Max hesitate over the linguistic parameters menu. "I'm not sure. It's like Rick—I know it has a meaning, but I don't know it because everyone just says the word." When Rick had asked about the human origin of the translation Max had provided, Max had blathered about how it was a common name and often assigned to those in charge and Rick had been the boss. He might have even mentioned *Magnum P.I.*, but given Rick's general insecurity about the universe's prejudices, he wasn't about to bring up *Rick and Morty*. "It's probably related to Homo sapiens."

"Query. Define Homo sapiens."

"Um... upright man or thinking man... something like that." Sometimes Max was embarrassed about how much he didn't understand about his own planet and his own language. When he'd been in school, the formal definition of Homo sapiens seemed like the sort of useless and stupid question a teacher would put on a test to catch kids who hadn't read the chapter. Max filed that sort of trivia in a part of the brain that got flushed regularly.

Rick made a bubbly, spitty sound and several smaller tentacles undulated, suggesting the irony of the name amused him.

"Yes, yes. I know. The rest of the universe believes humans are morons. However, we don't describe ourselves that way."

Rick's tentacles stilled and then several drew up closer to the bottom of his bulbous head. "Others' peoples call Rick's people the Ugly peoples."

Max's hands stilled over the controls. He turned and studied Rick's eyes. "They call you Uglies?" He blew out a breath and Rick's tentacles curled tighter. "Can I shoot all the bastards that insulted you like that? I'll aim for non-vital organs." Max intended that as a jocular form of emotional support, but all of Rick's arm tentacles balled up and the fingers along the undersides waved madly.

"I prefer you not shooting."

Max caught the nearest tentacle and drew it closer. "I didn't mean that. Sometimes humans exaggerate to show emotion. I exaggerated my potential action to show the depth of my anger that anyone would call you ugly. I won't shoot them. I'll just fantasize about shooting them. Often."

Slowly Rick's tentacles uncurled. "Unclear fighter humor is killing of people."

Despite the mangled translation, Max did understand the sentiment. He wound his arm around several tentacles and leaned toward Rick. "I would not kill over words. I only express depth of emotion."

Rick leaned back and for a time they sat quietly. "Unboned tentacle is clearer gauge of emotion than liar words."

Max laughed. "Probably." He had explained facial expressions to Rick, but those subtle clues were much harder to read than tentacle positions. Rick projected everything he felt. Max wondered if the other aliens said such mean things because they could see it bothered Rick's people or if they simply didn't care. They'd found Max a social worker of sorts, so they had some sort of moral code, but kindness didn't seem part of it.

In the weeks, or even months, Max had been on that first military ship, the crew had fed him and shown him how to piss in a retractable trough. However, they'd spent almost no time reassuring him or trying to improve communication. They were assholes, or as Rick would've said, polonium-headed poop people.

"What do the pirates who invaded call their people?"

Rick was silent for so long that Max was about to rephrase the question with a "Query" when Rick spoke, "Others' peoples cannot pronounce."

"How would it translate?"

"People who hunt."

"Of course." Max grunted. "They don't hunt well, though, do they?"

"They hunt well; humans hunt better."

Max ran a hand up and down a tentacle before he turned to work his magic on the translation computer. "Request. Say the name of pirate species."

Rick moved back to his position leaning against Max's back and burped a name.

The computer started "Peop—" Max typed a command. "Request. Repeat name." Rick did and this time the computer voice said, "Hunters." Max grinned and held a hand up. Rick obliged with a tentacle version of a high-five.

"Clever Max not from moron species as others suggest," Rick said, and Max imagined his whale song and burps sounded a little smug.

"Hell, yes."

"Clarify. Yes you believe you are from moron species. Option. Yes you are not from moron species."

"Yes, you are right that humans are clever," Max explained.

Rick's tentacles twitched. "Max is clever. Humans are disturbing."

Yeah, they had watched too many transmissions from Earth, but on the bright side, Rick had finally gotten to see *Star Wars*. He still loved Darth Vader, but had developed an unhealthy affection for Jar Jar. Max pulled up pictures of aliens he had seen on the military ship. He started with a tall alien with a huge upper lip and too many nostrils. Rick immediately offered a name, which the computer translated as "People."

"How do they describe themselves?" Max prompted.

"Unknown."

Max had learned that for Rick, that might mean he didn't know, but it could also mean he didn't have first-hand knowledge. "Query. Does anyone know?"

"Others' people say they were sure of aloneness and distressed at finding spaceships passing planet because they called themselves the chosen ones. They no longer believe in chosenness."

"Yeah, well 'Chosen' sounds like a good species name. So, when you're talking about your own species, what do you call yourself?"

The computer offered the ever-helpful translation, "The people from the planet of the people." Max smothered a curse. Before he could ask, Rick said, "Others' peoples call us as Uglies. We describe ourselves as ones who hide. Our planet is hidden."

"The Hidden People. That sounds like a proper name," Max said. It was sure as hell better than calling Rick's people the Uglies, especially since they weren't ugly. Once Max had gotten used to tentacles in general, it wasn't so strange to have a creature more tentacle than head, and the colors were beautiful. He loved Rick's streaks of beige through minty green and his orangey-red tentacle tips. He loved Kohei's streaks and spots and James's white patches, and he loved Xander's red tentacle tips, which his brothers envied. "Who owned the port where we first met?"

"Every peoples. I cannot land ship on planet owned by one peoples."

Max spun around so fast he jerked on a couple of tentacles and dragged Rick closer. "What?"

"Clarify. Area requiring clarification?" Rick was so damn calm, but Max's blood was near boiling point. The assholes had segregated Rick's people. They wouldn't allow him to land on their planet because they were convinced that Rick's people were ugly. Max was reconsidering his position on shooting these assholes. Unfortunately, Rick was too forgiving. And now Rick wanted to take them back into a universe full of polonium-headed poop faces.

"Never mind." Max pulled Rick closer and caught as many of his tentacles as he could in a hug. The rest of the universe might be judgmental and insane, but Max would make up for it by giving Rick the cuddles he loved.

Chapter Two

A new day brought a new opportunity for family drama. Max was assaulted as he came out of the secured door to the upper levels. "Max Father, I made new adjustment!" James waved a plastic part in the air.

"What is that a new version of?" Max reached for the model. According to Rick, the children were all precocious. He speculated it was because he had added too many nutrients to the gestation pool, but Max had another theory. Maybe Rick's people underestimated the value of parenting, but Max didn't. He knelt in front of James and turned the model in his hands. While all the children had grown, James was half his father's size. Ironically, Xander was only a few inches shy of Rick, but he still had an unusual lean look while James and Kohei were still cute and round. While only months old, they acted like teenagers, so Max tried to avoid using words like "cute" around them.

James ran a tentacle tip over the plastic model. "I applied your theory on focus of weapon," he said. "New mechanics provides control over intensity of directionality."

"Wow! You did?" He stuffed down a little bit of hurt that James hadn't waited for him when it was their shared project. He understood being excited, and James did lack patience. "Have you tested it?"

James's tentacles sagged. "My replicator only makes plastic prototype. Max Father, make alloy version, query?" James curled his manipulative little tentacles around Max's wrist.

"If either Rick Father or Xander check your numbers, I'll run a copy for testing," Max said. He didn't have the skills required to check the math. Hell, he wouldn't have made a plastic copy without running the design past someone.

"Rick Father never looks." James was definitely whining now.

"Rick Father is busy. You ask Xander to look at your numbers and if Rick Father is available, I will show him. Put the schematics on the computer."

James's tentacles squiggled and curled, but Max stood. He would not be emotionally blackmailed by a six-month-old. Much. "I hope it works out. I would love to carry a weapon we designed together," Max said.

All James's tentacles twitched and stretched. "I'm talking at Xander!" Sadly, James was probably using that "at" accurately. Xander was best at languages, but James talked more. A lot more.

Max chuckled. Xander should check the numbers because Rick had been busy. His navigational program went far beyond Max's simple ability to understand math, but he did understand it would make travel safer and cheaper. How it did that was a little less clear. After all, Max had only gone through advanced calculus and differential equations for his engineering degree. In the wider universe, that gave him a toddler-level math expertise.

It bothered Max that James focused so much of his greater mathematical genius toward weapons. That pirate attack had changed him.

The door to the computer room was closed, so Max activated the light and settled in to wait. Sometimes Rick was too busy to notice things like doors or invading pirates. However, Max hadn't even pulled up his latest computer program on his tablet before the door slid open. Rick's tentacles were at half-curly fry, but when he saw Max, they all stretched out.

"Max." Rick curled tentacles around Max's wrist and pulled him into the room. The door closed behind him, and Rick began his turning ritual. He glided around Max, touching bare skin—an ankle here, an elbow there. In humans, touch created oxytocin, and Rick's circling probably did something biological because he loved doing it. Max turned in a slow circle the opposite direction until they were face to very large eye again.

Then Rick slid one of his smallest tentacles across Max's lips. A shiver went down Max's spine. Rick then leaned his head into Max's chest. "I incorrectly assumed James aggravation."

Max smiled. "He does want to test out a new weapon part."

Rick made a sound like bubbles, which was usually a good sign. Maybe he would have time to help James with the work. "Many testing of many parts."

"True."

Rick glided toward the main computer. "I am testing of navigation computer. I have no tentacles unburdened with tasks."

"That's fair." Max sat on the stool that had appeared in the room after he had started visiting. "I told him to ask Xander to check his work."

"Kohei must should work more math." Rick was right. However, Rick never voiced his opinions to the boys, and Max wasn't going to get involved in this case. Kohei was far more interested in physical tasks, and Max didn't want to force the kids to do something they hated. His father had tried to get him involved in business, and that had not ended well. Max wondered how they were handling the violence that had followed the Nish invasion of Earth space. Luckily, the United States was faring better than some areas. They had more suicide pacts in fringe churches than rioting.

Max's message had done less to calm those waters than he had hoped.

He'd told Earth they were safe, and the evening news proceeded to obsess over how unsafe they all were. And the irony was that the rest of the universe was unlikely to ever wander into Earth territory again. It was too far out—and on an arm of the galaxy that the aliens didn't care about. Earth was in the older half of the Milky Way and space-faring species had decamped and headed for the half of the galaxy that was still forming new stars. When humans finally got to space, they were going to find much of their part of the galaxy was devoid of heavy metals because it had already been mined out.

The computers reported that the engines were running. "Where are we going?" Max asked.

"I require compensation for supplies necessary to running of our ship." Rick had repeated that phrase often enough in the last week that Max was getting suspicious. Usually Rick was quick to share information, and the improved translation matrix meant they should be able to discuss navigation.

"Clarify require."

"Require. Develop need for lacking resource." Rick kept his main eye focused on the computer. He sucked at lying, even lying by omission.

"So, we're out of money?" Max translated.

"Query. Clarify 'out.'"

"Out. Clarification. Supplies have been depleted. We are devoid of money. All remaining supplies are outside of our control."

Rick hesitated long enough to suggest Max was not going to like his answer. "Out is hyperbole. We are limited in resources," Rick said. "Critical alloys depleted. Fuel restricted."

That sounded more dire than Max had expected. He put James's model to one side. "Can I do something to assist with gathering resources?" After all, Max had used a number of those alloys to fabricate weapons and armor to counter the known attack strategies of the most violent of the aliens he'd read about in the database. If the Hunters or Nish or even the Pajekh chose to attack, Max had his countermeasures ready.

Rick's tentacles curled. "I don't want you to earn compensation. I can earn compensation without...." The sentence ended with a series of belches. It had been a while since that had happened.

"Translation matrix failure," Max said.

Rick's tentacles twitched and curled again, so this issue was seriously upsetting him. "Max possible not risk life as warrior."

"Oh." Max blew out a breath as he realized what Rick feared. "I don't have to take a job fighting."

Instead of reassuring Rick, that made his tentacles curl up tighter.

Max had clearly misinterpreted that bit of word soup. "Rick, what do you not want?"

"Translation matrix failure. Negative contradiction with desire."

That was still annoying. "Query. What do you fear?"

Rick was silent for so long that Max wondered if he didn't understand or if Max had crossed some cultural line. The question seemed simple enough to understand. Rick inched closer and said, "Irrational dislike Max surrogate for not-Rick." Rick's tentacles curled tighter. "Irrational. Rational, Max earns compensation the way Max chooses."

Max held out his hand and waited until Rick wrapped a tentacle around his wrist. The tiny tentacles along the underside tangled with Max's fingers. "Clarification. Irrational dislike of relationship with others is jealousy. You are jealous. I would be jealous if you chose another to be surrogate of future offspring."

The tiny finger tentacles undulated. "Others do not father like Max."

"I take that as a compliment," Max said. "Not that I'm ready to have more children now," he added quickly. When it came to communication, it was best to be direct.

"Ship is too small for additional offspring," Rick said, even though most of the ship consisted of empty crew quarters. On the other hand, the kids did tend to get into everything. Rick restricted them to the lower decks, otherwise James might have disassembled something more important than a secondary fabricator. However, it worked once James and Xander had reassembled it, which was impressive. "I am jealous of other surrogate Max compensation."

"Then I will not surrogate... or fight." That did limit his job opportunities. Max's guidance counselor had not prepared him for this. He felt a little sympathy for Buffy who was a great slayer, but a pretty sucky breadwinner. Some skills didn't transfer into the job market, and psychotic father willing to kill for offspring apparently fit into the same category as vampire slayer. "I could sell translation matrix," he suggested. When they'd been at the docks, it hadn't seemed like a viable option, but Max wanted to bring some money in.

"They think of human as language of morons." Rick slipped a tentacle under Max's shirt and caressed his skin. Despite Rick's concern, Max didn't care what others thought. It wasn't as if these aliens had impressed him with their brilliance. They'd "rescued" Max from his jet and then ignored or terrorized him for weeks on that military ship, all without trying to have any meaningful conversation.

"We could prove that humans aren't morons. We could introduce them to the polonium-headed idiots who tried to steal from us." Max smiled at the thought of the pirates having to explain that one human had kicked their asses. They called their species "Hunters," but one pilot had taken them all out.

Rick's tentacles quivered with happiness, and Max laughed. Rick had a not-so-buried mean streak when it came to the pirates. He knew that would cheer Rick up.

"Okay, I wouldn't do that, but, query, is there a way to convince people that humans are equal to other species?"

"Humans fail equality. They fail building spaceships."

That was a stupid way to judge others, especially when most other species assisted each other in reaching space. According to the records, the species Max's social worker belonged to had helped dozens of younger species, and they often allied themselves with younger races. It was like a galactic version of a pyramid scheme. Rick's species, and humanity, had simply been left out.

"We are working on spaceships. And most people don't know anything about humans. How hard would it be to convince them they needed to know English? Those pirates believed I was worth listening to."

Rick pulled Max closer and curled more tentacles around him. "Max is worth listening to most always. Other species will not respect Max or listen to any of the Hidden People. Warrior species language worth money but humans never never seen warrior by others peoples."

"I dislike other people," Max complained.

"Agreed," Rick quickly responded. "They last chance markdown the skills Max offers." Rick said. He had heard too many commercials, but Max got the point. If the universe was some version of *Glee*, he would happily play the part of Santana Lopez and show these people what a real bitch could accomplish.

"Maybe you can sell the linguistic database for me."

"The other peoples' special markdowns applies to all the work of the Hidden Peoples. My program is worth..." whale song. "They give..." more whale song.

Max frowned. That did not sound good. "Translation matrix failure." Max needed a way to judge relative value because the damn translation matrix always screwed up money, even if raw numbers were easy to program. Weird computer. "Query. How does the value of your program compare to the value of your ship?" he finally asked.

"Linguistic smart Max," Rick unwound his tentacles and backed away. "My program is worth two and one-quarter ships." Max was impressed. *Damn.* Max could hear the comedian Fluffy saying that in his exaggerated tone because that was a hell of a lot of money. Rick continued. "However, the special markdowns the Hidden Peoples suffer mean I will receive one-fifth of ship."

"Wait. What?" Shock made focusing on the numbers difficult.

"Query. What what?" Rick was calm, as if getting cheated out of most of his money was normal.

Max closed his eyes and silently counted to ten. "Query. Who gets your money?"

"Only I and Max have access my money." Rick untangled all but one tentacle and squeezed Max's wrist.

Max sighed. "Query. What person gets the compensation you are denied because of special markdowns?"

"Brokers hire access to Hidden Planet. They pay to government for access to Hidden Planet market. Those people take trade items and get compensation on trade planets." Again, the calm tone left Max in shock. Unfortunately, this wasn't a problem Max could shoot, although he wanted to.

"Why don't you go to a trade planet yourself?" If Rick was afraid of the other aliens, Max was more than willing to play bodyguard, and he might even consider a career in breaking knees—assuming he could find something that passed as a knee on whichever alien insulted Rick.

"The many peoples refuse compensation to Hidden People."

Max thought about how his social worker had reacted to Max's decision to take the job with Rick. Even then he'd known something more important than the volume of Rick's voice was involved. "Query. How can they refuse to trade? Query. Isn't refusing trade unfair?"

Rick shifted to look out of different eyes. "Query. Is fairness required for earning of compensation?"

Max blew out a frustrated breath. Rick had him there.

Rick shifted closer and Max spread his knees so Rick would fit between them. "Hidden People are hidden. Hidden Planet is hidden. The peoples dislike hidden. They retaliation."

"Clarify. They retaliate," Max said absent-mindedly. "Query. What do they retaliate against?"

"Answer. The hidden."

One of these days Max was going to pound his head against a wall. However, ignoring communication problems had gotten him knocked up last time, so he had to put on his big-pilot's pants and figure this out.

"Query. Why do they care if you are hidden people?"

Rick turned a quarter rotation, which almost always meant he was confused. Or worried. Sometimes it meant worried. "The Hidden People disrupt space..." and another series of belches and wails came through the computer. Rick continued despite the translation failure. "The peoples cannot ship navigate that part of space without..." More wailing.

"Wait." Max caught Rick by the tentacle. "Query. Have the Hidden People set up a defense that blocks other people from traveling in their part of space?"

"Yes." Rick didn't even twitch a tentacle.

Oh, that explained most of the anger. Rick's people wouldn't let the others walk on their metaphorical lawn. And the others were retaliating by putting sanctions on the Hidden people. That made a lot more sense than discrimination against non-symmetry. However, if these assholes thought they could cheat Rick, they had another thought coming. Max had no idea how to fix this, but he did know the universe did not get to cheat his husband or his children.

Max was distracted when a tentacle snuck under his shirt. "You are horny." Max was not complaining at all.

"Lack of horns," Rick disagreed. "But I am the man your man could smell like."

Max snorted so hard that he had a snot backup on the brain. "You like those deodorant commercials too much."

"I am desired as is man of muscles." Rick raised a tentacle to mimic flexing an arm. The gesture was ridiculous when gym rats did it, and doubly so when Rick copied it, but Max had to agree with Rick's basic conclusion. Rick was hot. Max caught that red tipped tentacle.

"Tangle tentacles." Rick curled a tentacle around Max's wrist and tugged him off the awkward stool. It was funny how Max had learned to interpret tentacle positions, even in the absence of any emotional tone. The translator was still monotone despite everything Max had done, but Rick's happiness shone through. The finger tentacles tickled across Max's arm before Rick wound the slender tentacle around Max's hand.

"You have beautiful tentacles to tangle." Max hooked his heel around one of Rick's larger tentacles and pulled it closer. Rick twitch-shivered in pleasure. Then Rick grabbed Max's legs and jerked them hard enough that Max lost contact with the floor. But Rick had the strength to hold him, so now Max was suspended as Rick slowly spread his legs.

"You can't get my pants off that way," Max warned. Their sex did lead to a significant amount of torn clothing.

Rick tugged the bottom of Max's shirt, pushing it up. It got caught on Max's neck, and trapped his arms in the fabric. Maybe that was an accident, maybe not. But Rick took advantage of the situation to curl around Max's bare torso. Fingers pulled at Max's nipple, and his cock hardened.

"No fair," Max complained, his voice muffled in his shirt.

"All advantage fair in love," Rick countered. He pulled Max's legs up.

Max squirmed out of his shirt and grabbed the nearest tentacle. He knew Rick was strong enough to hold him. Hell, they'd had wall sex as often as they'd had sex in a bed, but some instinctive part still made Max struggle to get his feet under him. "You cheat," Max said when a tentacle slid down his ass crack.

"Happily." Rick popped Max's fly open while tickling the edge of his hole and untying his shoes and tossing the shirt away. Max did appreciate a lover who could multitask.

"It's not fair. You have too many tentacles for me to keep up with." Max caught the thickest of Rick's arm tentacles. It was shorter than the others with fatter fingers on the underside. And Max knew from experience that he could drive Rick wild by playing with it.

Max gasped as Rick counterattacked with a quick thrust into his ass. Then the little bastard curled the end of his tentacle against Max's prostate. Losing control of his reactions, Max arched his back and clutched at whichever limbs were closest. Rick took the opportunity to yank Max's pants off.

"You dirty bastard," Max said with a gasp.

Rick hesitated long enough for Max to twist around in search of that vulnerable tentacle. "I am going to turn you into a ball of twitching tentacles."

Drawing Max close, Rick blew bubbles against Max's stomach. "Clarify. I make you spill genetic materials prior temporally." He pressed Max's prostate again, and Max writhed as tentacles held him tightly. However, he was a man on a mission, and he had to focus. He reached for the thick tentacle again, but another tentacle wrapped around his wrist and pulled his arm down to his side. Max was planning his counterattack when Rick pressed in, forcing Max's hole to stretch.

Max gasped. "Are you?" He swallowed the rest of his words. His hole strained as a second tentacle pushed in next to the first one. That meant a tight coil undulated against Max's prostate as he forced a tentacle farther into Max's body . Max arched his back and moaned as he struggled to accommodate both tentacles.

"No longer mutually exclusive options. Rick problem solve winning for partner twitching." Rick tightened his hold on Max's thighs before his tentacle surged forward.

Max screamed in pleasure. It was like a too-hot shower, like the burn of stretching sore muscles, like the tightness at the end of a marathon. It was good—so intense that it edged toward pain, and yet left Max wanting more. "You fucking cheater," Max gasped the words.

"I fucking," Rick agreed with deep and full belches. Tentacles undulated against Max's stomach, against the backs of his legs where he was ticklish, against his trapped arm. Then Rick's reproductive tentacle touched his nipple before curling like a cinnamon bun on Max's chest.

"Oh, you—" Max screamed and writhed as the suction started. Rick sucking so hard that Max's nipple felt as if it was being pierced, something Max had been stupid enough to try at eighteen. Then he gentled the pressure to feather kisses over the abused nub. Rick alternated the two until Max thought he couldn't take more. He writhed. Only then did Rick gentle his motions to soft strokes.

"Yes, I." Rick proclaimed.

Even though the reproductive tentacle was within reach, Max couldn't gather his thoughts long enough to make a grab at it. His cock was too hard for him to think about anything other than coming. Damn aliens with their damn tentacles.

One of the tentacles in his ass pressed farther in, a hard point of lust and need. But at the same time, Rick's other tentacles supported Max's body, teasing with tickle-touches. The contrast left Max feeling like one giant, overly exposed nerve.

Rick curled his tentacles around Max's fingers and wrist, and Max tightened his hand. That made Rick shiver, and Max tightened his legs around Rick's walking tentacle. That sent a larger shiver through him, and all his tentacles shimmied, including the two up Max's ass.

Max lurched forward as much as he could while still wrapped in a tangle of Rick's limbs. The movement loosened Rick's hold over Max's hand, and Max grabbed a tentacle the way he would a rope when trying to climb it. He circled the tentacle until it was wrapped around his forearm and then he grasped it tightly. The move never failed to turn Rick into a mass of quivering octopus, and it didn't fail this time. Rick pressed his mouth against Max's shoulder and blew air. Sometimes that sound meant amusement, but when they were tangling tentacles, it had a whole different meaning.

Lust distracted Rick, and normally Max would've used the momentary distraction to grab that reproductive tentacle to drive Rick crazy until he was a pile of goo. However, his ass was stuffed so full that every move increased the pressure on his prostate. Rick recovered before Max could mount a counterattack or even figure out how to think straight while he was impaled.

Rick's fingers teased the inside of Max's thighs before moving in toward his balls.

"You're killing me." Max let his head fall back, and a tentacle wrapped around his neck before the red tip teased Max's lips. At the same time, a tender touch explored his cock and a tentacle curled around it. Max tried to thrust, but Rick held him suspended in tentacles, with the weight of both of them supported only by his walking tentacle. Max's boyfriend was one muscled geek.

"Never kill Max. Never, never, never." Rick whispered the words against Max's skin. Each belch made air dance over Max's skin.

"Then move," Max begged. He had lost this round, and he was willing to embrace his inner loser if Rick would move his tentacles. At one point, Rick had been so unsure of himself. He had probably feared how a warrior would react to Rick showing off his strength, so their playful competition... Max felt the bonds of trust developing between them.

And Max would win later. He would reduce Rick to quivering limbs and then jerk off all over his red-tipped tentacles. But right now, he couldn't focus on Rick—not when his ass was stuffed so full that he couldn't get his brain to work.

Rick tightened his hold of Max's cock while pushing farther up Max's ass at the same time.

Pleasure slammed Max like Hulk Hogan taking out an opponent. He writhed as Rick slipped a tentacle into his mouth. The salty musk that was uniquely Rick filled his senses, and Max sucked on it.

Rick quivered, and the resulting vibration in his ass and around his cock gave Max the final push he needed. He came with a scream. Rick must have enjoyed himself too because his limbs were nearly as warm as the hot body pressed against Max's chest. That only happened with good sex.

Rick shimmied.

"Max skilled in maximizing pleasure," Rick said with a rumble. "Maximized skilled in maximizing pleasure. Maximized maximizing skilled in maximizing maximized pleasure."

Max laughed. That was the nicest compliment he'd had since someone called his intestines asymmetrical. "And you make me happy for stagnant water. I would stagnate in this water every day for the rest of my life and be maximum happy."

Rick slowly pulled his tentacles out of Max's body. "Stagnant waters sometimes are beautiful," Rick agreed.

Max's bare feet touched the floor. Max drew Rick closer. Rick's tentacles danced over Max's skin, and Max held on tighter. This was perfect. He wished he didn't have to deal with the rest of the universe. He had his one alien and that was all he wanted or needed. Well, except of course for the children, but Max tried very hard not to think about the children when his brains had recently leaked out of his cock.

Chapter Three

Max threaded his way through the crowd, wondering why aliens hadn't yet invented mass transit. Sure, he had issues with the New York subway system, and falling asleep on a train that was bound for Tremont had not been a fond memory. However, someone could make a killing with a tentacle-friendly bus route.

He looked at the towers that rose in the distance. He wondered if the city was as crowded as the docks. Maybe he'd find out later. Right now he had a mission.

A large bell-shaped alien crashed into Max and cut between him and Rick. Max cursed the asshole's backside and reached for Rick. Rick hesitated, but Max kept his hand out, waiting for Rick to get over whatever insecurities made him want to avoid touching in public. Rick might fear giving Max some sort of ugly cooties, but Max didn't listen to bullies in high school and he sure as hell wasn't going to start now. If he could survive being gay in the damn Midwest, he could survive holding tentacles with his non-symmetrical partner.

"Others reinforced in belief Max from moron people," Rick warned him in a whisper even as he slipped a tentacle into Max's hand.

"I don't care." Max squeezed Rick and turned to wade into the crowd again. This time Rick pressed close, his tentacles brushing Max's back.

A more honest answer would have been that Max cared a lot, but he was too stubborn to ever let someone else intimidate him into changing. No one liked being the butt of the joke, the outcast, the loser who was afraid of going into the boys' locker room after school. However, when Max had come out of the closet after Don't Ask, Don't

Tell had ended, he'd sworn to himself that he would never go back in again. And he wouldn't. If the universe didn't like his relationship with Rick, well he was all out of fucks. Being the victim of alien abduction did that to a man.

Rick gave him a gentle push to the right and Max spotted the map. They had a distorted point of view that meant straight roads appeared to curve inward toward the middle and none of the data was communicated in text that could be translated. It used a series of hard-to-memorize symbols.

He couldn't find the symbol for Trader. "Query. Where is the trader we discussed?" Max asked.

"Query. Clarify. Time or content of discussion."

Max glanced around at the passing crowd and then leaned closer to whisper, "Clarify. The trader who couldn't get permission to trade on the Hidden World."

Rick rotated a few degrees and aligned his largest eye with Max's face without answering. Seconds passed, and Max waited. Unless he missed his guess, Rick was questioning Max's intelligence. Either that or he was getting cold tentacles. Finally Rick said, "Reminder. Those with no license on Hidden World are those who will not trade with those of Hidden World. The others maintain interconnected anger at the Hidden People."

"They can be interconnected in their anger all they want," Max muttered. As far as he was concerned, a universe that boycotted a species for being secretive deserved to get their tentacles handed to them on a platter, and Max was the guy to do it. He grew up watching *Mission Impossible* and the *A-Team*. He had a plethora of cheesy revenge plots to draw on. "This guy is a trader, and that means he wants to make a profit."

Rick slid his tentacle forward so the tip escaped Max's grip and curled around his wrist. "Agreed. Compensation is significant motivation for those motivated by compensation."

Either Rick was trying to be pithy or the translation matrix needed help distinguishing different versions of that word. "I plan to take advantage of his desire for compensation," Max said. And if this guy wanted Rick's fancy new navigation software, he would have to assist them in a little Nathan Ford-esque plotting. Max might not live up to the standards set by the mastermind of *Leverage*, but he was willing to try.

"Query. Which what advantage of compensation?"

That had been clear as mud. "Do you trust me?" Max asked. He didn't have the detailed language needed to explain how his plan would come together, and he definitely didn't want to try in the open.

Several of Rick's tentacles snapped up into tight curls. "Clarification. Any action that is set leads to your belief in my mistrust is unintended." He reached for Max with several tentacles as though seeking to reassure him.

Max smiled and ran his fingers along the underside of a tentacle. The tentacle in question shivered. "Clarify. Sometimes humans in a relationship will ask that question, not to seek information, but to remind a partner that trust is valued."

Rick's tentacles uncurled again. "My memory exceeds humans who must forget. I trust Max."

"It's not that humans forget." Max struggled for the right words. "Sometimes we hurry to speak or act and our brain doesn't pull up all relevant information."

Rick made a sound like blowing bubbles. "Humans are odd," he announced.

"I couldn't agree with you more. One of these days you're going to meet some other humans, then you're going to discover exactly how odd we are."

Rick made a quarter turn so the tentacle wrapped around Max's wrist was pulled tight. Maybe he was questioning the likelihood of humans finding space, but Max put a little more faith in his species.

Sure, they were a disorganized mess of suicide cults and rioting now, and they would be a disorganized mess of crime and drama once they arrived, but he suspected that in the middle they would pull their shit together.

That was what happened when people were pushed. They adapted, they survived. In SERE training, instructors had told Max that humans could survive the impossible, and had on a semi-regular basis. They'd proved that with a gruesome, full-color proof. In this case, Max figured the visit from alien ships was a serious gut shot, but the human race was going to fight back eventually.

They would get up to space if only so they could properly scream at the law enforcement officers for chasing the Nish through their gravity well. And then they would sue someone. Max worried that the universe would do the same thing to him that it had done to Rick and judge him by his people. He just had to make sure that his reputation was settled first. Max walked in the direction Rick had suggested when he'd touched the map, and Rick followed.

He hadn't been thinking about reputations when he'd been on that law enforcement patrol ship. Back then he had taken every opportunity to embarrass himself. He was fairly sure they had tranquilized him a couple of times because his general level of panic had gotten too high, but in Max's defense, his survival and escape classes had never covered alien invasion. He assumed that was an oversight the military was addressing now.

"Query. Will Trader have access to language translation of the Hidden People?" Max asked. He'd worked his ass off to get that computer system to recognize English and if he had to start over with a different language, he might stab someone.

"Concern. Sharing of linguistic database could lead to illicit copying. He is known for removing without adequate compensation."

"A greedy businessman? Who would've thunk?" Apparently there were some constants in the universe.

Rick hurried to walk at Max's side instead of following. "Query. Clarify 'thunk'. Thunk is sound to fall."

"Clarify. Thunk is conjugation of think when speaker makes fun of himself."

Rick didn't say anything, but he had that expression again, the one that said that he questioned Max's sanity. Max was a bad, bad boyfriend because he found that entirely too entertaining. He cleared his throat. "I'm going to say some things to the trader that you might not understand. I am asking you to believe that I can outsmart our enemies."

"Correction. Trader is not enemies. Trader is seeker of compensation, not danger to eliminate."

Max tugged on Rick to pull him closer for a second. A lavender alien with big lips flinched away as if they were a pile of dog poop, and several of Rick's tentacles curled. That called for some serious distraction. Pulling out the big guns, Max ran his fingers up the largest central tentacle to the point where it met Rick's body. With a shiver, Rick let his tentacles drop again. "I'm not sure if I should be complimented that you think I'm capable of taking on the universe in armed battle or insulted that you're afraid I might."

A large alien came barreling past them on the walkway, nearly pushing them into the side of a building. Max not-so-accidentally stepped on a trailing tentacle. The creature gave a high-pitched yelp, but Max kept walking.

"Max bad," Rick said with a soft burble.

Max didn't bother answering. "Is that the trader's symbol?" Max pointed at the writing beside a door. The shops on the main level were the largest ones, with elevated walkways leading to smaller shops on the upper levels. So if this guy had a street-level shop, he was big-time. Max felt a little fizzle of worry that he might be biting off more than he could chew.

Rick didn't notice Max's unease because he simply said, "It is."

Max blew out a breath. Putting aside his worry, he stepped up to the door. He waited for the side of the door to retract, but nothing happened. He glanced at Rick. His tentacles weren't curled as much as tucked close to the central leg.

"Query. How do I get door to open?"

"Answer. Request entry without one of the Hidden People."

"Yeah, that doesn't work for me," Max said. "Query. Can we show him a small part of the programming, something that makes him want it?"

"Answer. Yes. Clarify. He will not trade with the Hidden People."

"I hate that you act like that's normal."

Rick just studied him for a good minute before he pulled a small computer display out of his hat and tapped on it. He let go of Max's wrist and glided forward before pressing his computer to the door. Max moved closer to the door. *Come on guy. Get curious. Or greedy.* Max could work with either one.

The computer next to the door beeped and hummed and chittered, but the door remained stubbornly closed. Max had almost decided to give up on this lead and look for someone else to act as their point man, but then the doors slid open a fraction of an inch.

Rick made a farting noise.

Hopefully that wasn't a sign. Because if this plan didn't work out, Max didn't have the screenwriters the *A-Team* folks did. He didn't get to reshoot the scene if these aliens decided to take offense at his attempt to reorder the universe, and Max had avoided researching alien penal codes and prison systems.

Chapter Four

Max studied the face peering up at him. It was a beige alien, one from a species he recognized from the law enforcement ship. It had dark lavender lips with wide, purpley stripes on the face. It made a high-pitched sing-song cry and the translator said, "Demand information." Max assumed that meant "what?" Rick pulled back, but Max tightened his grip on Rick's tentacle.

"I want to trade."

The alien at the door peered up at Max and stretched his long neck to stare at Rick. "Not trading."

Max turned and took Rick's computer out of his tentacle. If this trader didn't want the program, he wouldn't have opened the door. So he wanted to be talked into this. Max needed the right words. "This program is worth money. Compensation. Profit." Max wasn't sure if the words were getting across because the trader stared blankly. But he hadn't slammed the door yet. Rick slipped a tentacle under the waistband of Max's pants, but Max didn't dare break eye contact with the trader—not even to tell Rick to stop molesting him.

The trader stood straighter, stretching out to his full five-feet-high. After he looked around the street behind Max, his gaze settled on Rick. "Behind," he said in a screeching voice, and then he retreated into his shop and the door closed with a sharp snap.

Max blew out a breath and turned to Rick. "That went well."

Rick tilted his head to the side. "I question your use of language."

"So did my English teacher," Max admitted. "So, where is the back door on this place?"

"Suggestion. We return to the ship." Rick tugged at Max's wrist.

The rainbow of aliens walking past them represented every color and a huge range of sizes, but all of them were united in being assholes to Rick's people. And here he had believed Roddenberry's promise that space and the future would be better. At least he didn't have to battle any Borg. "Would Darth Vader return to the ship?" Max asked. When all else failed, he found Rick reacted well when Max appealed to Rick's favorite sith. And Vader never retreated.

"He would hire for compensation to build poorly engineered war machine," Rick said. "I lack funds of compensation and would avoid Death Star death." He tightened his hold on Max's wrist.

"Right." Max couldn't fault the logic. "Suggestion. We find the back entrance and sell your program."

Rick's tentacles twitched, but he started walking away. "Darth Vader failed in quality-checking death machines."

"I agree. One really good engineer could have fixed most of his problems."

"One good engineer created problems. The Hidden People welcome Galen Erso as good at hiding." Rick waved a couple of smaller tentacles.

Max wasn't sure how one person could have both Galen Erso and Darth Vader as personal heroes, but then no one was perfect. If that was Rick's worst trait, Max would survive. Rick led them through an arched opening into some sort of covered walk or alley. Grates ran along the sides of the walk.

Rick turned down another alley, this one larger. Almost no one was around and vehicles glided along rails without any drivers. So this was for deliveries.

"Current action causes distress."

Max stopped. "I don't want to push you to do something you don't want to."

Rick moved closer. "You do not exert force or pressure on me."

"If you want to go back to the ship, you should go back."

Rick rotated a quarter turn. "Query. Do you wish to return to ship?"

Max sighed. He felt like he was reliving the same fight he'd had with every boyfriend he'd ever dated. What do *you* want to do? I don't know; what do *you* want to do? One of the levels of hell was full of people refusing to express an opinion. But at the same time, Max was tempted to start that circle jerk of uncertainty. He wanted to give Rick room to make his own mind up. "I want to sell your program for fair compensation. I can request compensation without you coming with me."

"Clarify. You cannot. You fail providing required information regarding technical specifications."

That was probably true. Max sighed. "We can go back to the ship."

"Query. Do you wish to return to ship?" Rick traced lines on Max's arm.

"No," Max admitted, even though he felt guilty about saying it. He was an asshole for pushing Rick. Max had avoided marching for gay rights, so it felt hypocritical to metaphorically shove Rick out of the asymmetrical closet.

"As you tell offspring, I reserve right to call you polonium-headed poopy face." Rick walked down the alley, his largest arm tentacle still around Max's wrist.

"I am not a poop face," Max protested.

"Potentiality of poopy face exists," Rick said. Once again, his logic was on point. Rick stopped in front of a door. "Entrance to back for delivering of supplies."

"Clarify. Service entrance." Max stepped in front of the door and waited. The trader probably had surveillance, so now they could only wait; hope that he was curious enough about the program to open the door; pray that this scheme wasn't illegal or if it was, that they didn't get caught. Max was starting to regret his decision to avoid the criminal database.

After several minutes, the service door was flung open and the short trader stood in the opening. He sang loudly, and once again, his translator barked out, "Demand information."

"I want to sell you a computer program for navigation." Max took a deep breath and tried to ignore the flush of adrenaline that made his heart pound. Rick's tentacle tightened around his wrist.

The trader frowned at Max and then Rick and back again. "Species of you is inferior in navigation."

Once again, Max had found a logical alien. "The program is superior."

The trader made a shrill whistle that ended in a three-note trill that repeated several times. Max got the feeling he'd been cursed out by a flute. "Superior but ugly not traded."

"You can profit from trade without seeing ugly," Max said. That was a generality, but he didn't trust the translation computer with any sort of nuanced suggestion.

Rick spoke up, but the translator only caught about every third word. "Husband.... Computer program.... Others peoples.... Compensation.... Others peoples." The nouns were separated by burps and rumbles that made the trader stand taller with each passing second. Apparently Max had not done a good job of programming the translation computer with vocabulary related to conning people. However, the trader's gaze was darting back and forth like a spectator at a tennis match where both competitors had been dipping into the meth stash.

When Rick finished, the trader said, "Come," and retreated into his shop. Max traded looks with Rick and then they both followed.

"What did you tell him?" Max asked.

"Max lacks sense that moron species would possess."

Max snorted. That was probably true, but he still doubted Rick had said it, at least not to someone outside the family. When the offspring and Max ganged up to declare a water war on Rick, he said that and worse.

They followed the trader through shelving lined with numbered boxes into a room that resembled Rick's computer room.

"Business communication facilitator." The trader poked a long, boned finger toward a bright blue control unit.

Rick set his computer down on a ledge clearly built for it and tiny wires rose from the surface. Dozens slid into the cracks in the sides of the tablet. Hopefully that was normal. Rick didn't seem bothered, and he was very protective of it.

Rick reached a tentacle toward Max. "We can communicate more easily now."

Gone was the broken English, the almost right word choices, the awkward phrasing.

"What the hell happened with the translation computer?"

"Official translator functions as a business communication facilitator," the trader said. "Database is right that you are from species of morons who cannot leave their planet. You didn't make current navigation program." Max heard the anger in the computer-generated voice.

Ignoring the trader, Rick answered Max's question. "Every linguistic database in the known universe is entered, so the computer has a large enough sample to compare a new language against linguistically similar samples. Every species donates to one system. No one can tamper with one system. Only buy a license to use it."

Rick's voice still sounded like Rick—like the tones Max had assigned him on the translation computer. However, now the emotional content of the words was clear. Rick had a softness to his voice that his loud belches and rumbles hid and the computer voice had—up until this point—been missing. Max smiled. "It's impressive. I'm surprised no one has stolen the programming." Max was already wondering if he could scam someone out of a copy.

The trader interrupted, and the computer translated his impatient tone. "Programming can't be accessed or reproduced by examining externally various systems and their functions."

With one last smile for Rick, Max turned his attention back to the trader. "We call that reverse engineering. We look at the function and attempt to recreate the process. However, I don't know how you would stop someone from trying to create their own version."

"People try to create one, but they don't have access to facilitator's linguistic database," the trader said. He stepped up onto a platform so he was as tall as Rick, but he was still several inches shorter than Max. "If your people know to reverse engineer, then you have more technical sophistication than database suggests." He sounded suspicious.

"And what does the database suggest?" Max gave the trader his most charming smile.

The trader made another flute whistle. "It says you are simple, non-spacefaring race with limited intellectual capacity and almost no skills. It says the larger of the two known humans in civilized territory took job doing surrogate work for Ugly People."

Max's stomach knotted. Two. Who the hell else was running around the universe? Max wanted to ask, but he had an obligation to Rick first, and he would look for the other humans as soon as he taught these assholes a little respect. "Not Ugly People," he said firmly. "The Hidden People. And my people have a great respect for surrogates and an emotional attachment to children that should not be underestimated."

"Clarify," the trader demanded.

"If someone touches the children I surrogate for, the children I have helped raise, I am very likely to take a sharp object and remove one or two tentacles," Max warned.

"He killed pirates who were Hunters," Rick added.

The trader touched his computer. "I should add violent to database."

Max stepped forward quickly enough that the trader flinched away and fell off his stupid little platform. "I wouldn't say my people are violent by nature, but we certainly have an ability to defend what's ours. That's why I will not allow someone to cheat us on the price of this navigation program."

"The program is not yours."

"It is mine," Rick said. "We are husbands, so we share resources. It is, therefore, his."

"Demonstrate worth of this program," the trader demanded.

Rick manipulated his tablet's screen and code flashed on the main screen on the facilitator. The trader moved closer. He had tentacles that ended in long, boned fingers that he ran along the screen as he read the code. "This is exceptional level of sophistication."

Rick shrank as his leg tentacle curved. It wasn't a curl, but it was close. Max moved to his side, although he wasn't sure why the compliment would upset Rick.

"You could make excellent profit from that," Max said.

"I cannot buy work of one Ugly, Hidden People."

Rick straightened. "I have not registered my work."

"So I can be the seller of record," Max said. They needed a desperate trader for this step. Apparently the universe took copyright very seriously, so they needed someone to buy the program and help register the program to Max.

The trader moved around Max, giving him a wide berth. He stopped in front of Rick. "What would inspire you to offer without registering your work on program?"

Rick rose to his full height. "My faith in my husband. If you were to take what is mine, he would do great harm. He has killed."

Max cringed. That was not where he had wanted the conversation to go. However, Max had to back his play. The only way to get this guy to help was to convince him that he could make a good profit and that Max and Rick would take his secret to the grave. That required a united front. "If you try to steal Rick's program, I will take a very sharp object and shove it into a very tender body part. But, we have a proposition for you. One that might make us both wealthy."

"My continued ability to earn compensation requires that I not trade with Ugly, Hidden People. They have angered most of universe by claiming territories behind their world, territories they don't have right to."

"We do not claim," Rick protested. "We wish you not to fly through our space. We only prevent you from doing that."

"And that prevents people from reaching space behind your world. To navigate around requires extraordinary time. You know this." The trader turned to Max. "Do you understand how his people anger other peoples?"

This asshole was trying to drive a wedge between them. He was playing a con of his own. At least, that was what Max would have assumed if a human was trying to split a partnership. Max leaned against the computer and rested his hand on his weapon. "My people would congratulate him. In fact, we do tend to claim territory preemptively, sometimes when someone else is already standing on it. Don't look for me to get upset because the rest of the universe can't figure out how to get around their security system."

The trader whistled, and the computer translated with a whispered, "Fuck you." He then spoke louder. "I will not trade with Hidden, Ugly People. If I do, I will not have any customers. I need compensation beyond one trade."

"But what if your customers didn't know that a product came from one of the Hidden People? What if they believe the product came from a previously underestimated species that had been grossly misunderstood?" Max smiled and tapped the screen on Rick's tablet.

"You are not genius to create this."

"We could tell people I was."

"That would be untruthful."

"I'm okay telling a lie, especially when the people I'm lying to have mistreated my husband." Max held his breath. This was it. Either this trader helped him or he threw them out. Or he reported them, and what they were attempting to do was illegal. That was a possibility.

The trader looked at each of them, but his gaze settled on Max. "You wish to lie to entire universe."

"Yep."

Another fluting curse followed, but this time the computer didn't translate it. Max waited as the trader seemed to debate with himself. Rick slid to Max's side and wrapped a tentacle around Max's waist. "You have a square head," Rick said softly. It took Max a second to realize Rick had called him polonium-headed, although he had been nice enough to leave out the poop reference.

"Other traders will not believe moron species can write this," the trader said.

He wanted to do this. Max gave a verbal push. "I bet you could convince them."

"No." The trader curled his fingers into a fist. "I desire the power to lie to others, but there will be too many questions. I cannot answer questions."

"I can," Max said. "With Rick's help at least. If you work with me, I can convince your customers that I created this, and then you can pay me full price."

The room went silent. Rick didn't give a single burp, but his tentacles were drawn up into curled balls. That sent arrows of guilt straight to Max's gut, but he was doing this for Rick, so he ignored the feeling. Instead, he focused on the trader. They needed the man's connections, and they needed help setting up this scheme; however, whether he would help was up in the air. Max prayed that greed was as strong of a motivation for aliens as it was for humans, and he added a second prayer that the program was as valuable as Rick thought. There was something perverse about praying for help with lying and cheating the law, but if that was what it took, Max would do it.

After a long silence, the trader said, "How good are your people at lying?"

Max grinned. "We're champions. No one lies better." Rick's tentacles balled up tighter, and the trader whistled, but Max could already tell this con was a go.

Chapter Five

The trader escorted them up a long ramp into what looked like either a living space or a more posh office. Wide windows overlooked the docks, and their ship squatted in the distance. Despite the fact that the five of them rattled around in the huge space, the ship was one of the smaller ones lined up along the boardwalk. A swarm of small ground vehicles was pulling another vessel back to the launch pad, and it dwarfed theirs.

"Reasoning moron people," the trader said once the door closed behind the three of them. Rick's tentacles tightened around Max's wrist.

"Are we back to the poor translations?" Max asked.

Rick spoke. "Computer of human matrix lacks connection."

Ah. That was the problem. The trader touched a table and a familiar console rose out of the center. "There!" The trader said.

Rick slowly released Max's arm and carried the computer over to the console to reconnect the human translation matrix Max had worked on so many hours to the fancy-dancy business communication facilitator. Max triggered a personal recording device he kept on him for those times when he needed to record language and work on the translation later.

"The computer is attached," Rick said. With the improved translator, Max heard the worry in his voice. He took Rick's nearest tentacle in his hand.

"So let's talk about how to get a fair price for the best piece of navigation software you're ever going to see." At least Max assumed that description fit. Rick said it was remarkable programming, and Rick's insecurities did not lend themselves to empty bragging.

The trader sat on a curved bench and pulled all his tentacles up onto the seat. "If I were willing to conspire with such a lie, I could not make others believe that you are programmer." Now that the translation machine was turned on, the trader sounded snotty again.

"You couldn't now, no," Max admitted. He looked around, but he didn't see another bench. Aliens were really shitty hosts. If Max ever got independently wealthy, he was going to fly back to Earth, hire a whole ship full of southern grandmothers and Russian grandmothers and Greek grandmothers and turn the whole army of old women loose on the universe. They could shame and lecture aliens into having manners. Max gave up finding a comfortable spot and sat on the floor cross-legged. "But anyone who is good at lying knows that you have to put a lot of true words around the lie to make it all smell good." Rick moved to Max's back and leaned into his back.

"Most people do not use scent to identify accuracy of information. Smell is irrelevant."

Apparently the universe was full of Mr. Spocks. "I suggest we begin with something more believable." Max pulled his weapon out and put it on the floor in front of him.

The trader fell off the back of the bench and scrambled to get his tentacles under him. "No violence. People from world with no space travel have far too much violence."

Max had no idea if the trader was insulting Earth specifically or undeveloped civilizations in general, but either way, he had missed the point. "I'm showing you the weapon, not threatening you. This weapon is modified. I didn't like how inaccurate the previous weapon was and so I requested that someone help me with a few modifications. This weapon can be fired accurately, even over a long range without increasing the risk that it will rupture an interior wall," Max explained.

Since he was a warrior, it made sense for him to introduce himself as an inventor with an improved weapon. "It's much more accurate."

"What need is a more accurate weapon?" The trader went from arrogant to confused.

"Oh, I don't know. It could have something to do with criminals and pirates and people who board ships and steal things. I find it very convenient to have a weapon around when that happens." Some days Max could not figure aliens out.

The trader climbed back onto the bench. "Computer security on external ship sensors prevents that. No personal weapon is necessary."

Max took a second to give Rick a dirty look. "Well, sometimes sensors don't work," he said. Rick had the grace to curl a few of his smaller tentacles. Max took that as an apology, and he turned his attention back to the trader. "And sometimes you find you have to defend yourself. Considering that the local police force chased the Nish through my home planet's atmosphere, I know that you have criminals. And anywhere there are criminals, there is a need for better weaponry. And that's what this is." Max patted the gun.

"Weapon is uniquely superior," Rick added. He might not have been thrilled with the idea of running a con, but he was still doing his best to provide good backup. Funny, but he was a better boyfriend than any of the actual boys Max had ever dated.

"Peacekeepers invest in weapons. There is very low profit."

Max doubted that. Civilizations were always searching for better weapons, and traders were always interested in cheating someone out of profit. Max would let him strip the profit off the weapon if it meant they could get the universe to accept Max as an inventor. "Maybe the weapon will not bring the same profit as the navigation system, but if you convince everyone that I made the weapon, then they might believe that I am capable of making other improvements on your technology as well."

For a long time, the trader didn't answer. Rick pressed closer and Max's butt ached, but they continued to stare at each other. Eventually the trader said, "Very complicated. It would be easier to have Hidden, Ugly One return to Hidden Planet to find a dealer permitted to trade. Then have licensed trader contact me to trade so we all have profit."

Max hated this guy, but at least he was honest about only caring about profit. If Rick could get a fair price on his own planet, there wouldn't be any reason for complicated schemes. Max leaned forward. "You will not see a penny of profit unless you help Rick get a fair price. If you don't deal with us directly, we will make a deal that requires any trader to leave you out of any and all compensation." Max took his weapon off the floor and shoved it back into the custom holster.

"That is illogical!" That hit a nerve with the trader.

"No, that is vindictive," Max corrected him. "And by the way, the correlation between human and vindictive is very high."

"The hidden one requires compensation. He has ship registered to himself. Ships require resources to run them."

Rick twitched, but he didn't comment.

Max stood slowly. "Yes, ships are expensive. I'm thinking of taking up the transport business. After all, using his program I can move goods and people from one place in the universe to another much more quickly than anyone else. I can make a very good living, and enjoy giving all your competitors discounts while making you pay more. Human..." Max held up one hand. "Vindictive...." Max held his second hand up at the same height. Of course, Max had seen one too many episodes of *Firefly* to want to make his living that way. If they let strange people on their spaceship, they wouldn't know what kind of trouble they were dragging along. However, the trader couldn't know that.

He stood on top of his bench. "Hidden One could sponsor me on Hidden Planet. You sponsor application so that I can trade on Hidden World. I will offer far more compensation than other traders on Hidden World would offer you. That would be successful for profits."

"I think that's a no, especially since we have no guarantee that you would actually work with us after we got you the license. And, of course, you're assuming that we could get you a license, even if we wanted to." Max held out his hand to Rick. Without hesitation, Rick slipped his tentacles into Max's hand and rose on his central leg.

"I could not get license. Too few. Peoples do not like Hidden People and wish to minimize routes of profit."

"Embargo," Max said. "They have a partial embargo on your world, but they must recognize how good the Hidden People are at their work or they wouldn't let anyone trade there. That means the program is wildly valuable."

Max took a step toward Rick's computer, but the trader stepped between. "How does improved weapon function?"

"You want technical specifications?" Max could do that. "You use a pulsed plasma system. The narrow beam at the end of the weapon expands to create a shock wave that damages or kills everyone in the path of the weapon's fire. I took an idea my people had with the ionizing electro-laser, only I modified it to ionize a narrow beam then send the electrical current down that path. If you had twenty people standing in a line, I could kill one without doing more than giving the people on either side a mild shock."

Max wasn't sure how much of that translated. James's understanding of technology and Max's knowledge of Earth weapon's systems had allowed them to create the new weapon, and all Max needed to do was convince the trader that he could make himself look like an expert in weaponry. "I have the file on Rick's computer. We can register the improvements right now. You can buy the right to sell either the weapons or the plans for the weapons. But you need to introduce me to your buyers as someone new, someone who brings innovation to the table."

"What table?" the trader asked.

Max sighed. Aliens. They were annoyingly literal.

Rick said loudly, "Humans perceive tables where there are none and find fluids of the body gross and undesirable. Twenty thousand credits for the weapon."

"Five thousand. No one will purchase it. This is simple move toward establishing that humans are not morons."

"Humans are not morons!" Rick said in an offended, trumpeting voice.

Max rested his hand on Rick's mantle. "If you introduce me to buyers of weapons, I can impress them with the need to purchase weapons."

"Humans are not impressive." And there was the arrogant voice Max knew and hated. And here he thought that only people with ranks of lieutenant colonel and up could be that obnoxious. Apparently he was wrong.

"You introduce me, and I will impress them and get them to buy the weapons. You don't have to get involved at all."

"I have no profit in introducing my buyers to potentially useless designer of useless weapons. Five thousand credits."

"I'll make you a deal," Max said. "When we sell these weapons to your buyers, you can keep twenty percent of the sale as your profit for making the introduction."

"I need eighty percent. Buyers are more valuable than weapons design." The trader moved closer, which left Max wanting to grab the asshole and shake him until all his tentacles flopped. Maybe he was putting off some sort of aggravation vibes because Rick slid between them.

"Without weapons, buyers are not buyers because they do not buy. You may have thirty percent."

"Buyers always buy something. To risk displeasing buyers on untested weapon from a moron species is dangerous. I need seventy percent." The two of them continued fast-paced negotiations until they settled on the trader taking sixty-four percent of any sales.

As soon as they had reached that agreement, Rick retrieved his computer, and Max followed him back down the ramp. The trader pursued from a distance, giving Max the feeling that he didn't trust them not to steal merchandise on their way out.

They were outside in the humid air before Rick said anything. "Danger. Other peoples lack a desire for weapons. A diamond is forever; weapons are not."

"People want to defend themselves."

"Not with weapons bought from assumed moronic people."

"I can change their minds. People see what they want to see." If Max could offer them a good product, they would change their minds at light speed.

"I see you." Rick curled tentacles around Max's wrist.

"Awww. I love you too," Max said. Rick was a closet romantic. And it turned out that Max was too because he found he would've done anything and risked anything to get Rick the respect and compensation he deserved. And as a side effect, he wanted their children to have more opportunities in a universe that was a little less unfair than the one they'd been born into.

Funny enough, it turned out the universe wasn't all that different from Earth.

Chapter Six

Max was packing the equipment he wanted to take to the buyer meet-and-greet when Rick burst into their room all flailing tentacles and belches. "I dislike with vehemence," the computer translated. The computer voice was weirdly calm even though Rick was loud and a bit screechy.

Max sighed. "I understand that." The second he got the message that the trader wanted Max to come without Rick, he knew it was going to cause drama. Maybe Rick had never joined the military, but he understood what it meant to have someone's six.

"Dislike with very much vehemence," Rick added. His outer tentacles were all curled up.

"I know that. But the trader is right. If I have an adult Hidden One with me, people will figure out that I'm lying."

"No. You are not lying about creation of new weapon, so I can go with without fear of perception of lying."

Max sighed. Rick was, in his own way, being sweet and protective and supportive, but this time he was also wrong. The trader understood intergalactic politics and psychology. At least, Max assumed he did because it matched what Max knew of greedy, selfish, soul-sucking human beings. "They will assume you did the work even though James and I worked together."

"They are non-assuming with Xander, so they can non-assume with me."

Max went back to packing the samples he planned to take with him. If nothing else, maybe they could get resources to replace the ones he and James had spent on making the prototypes. "Xander is a child."

And boy wasn't that making Max feel guilty, but he needed help. Since Xander spoke English even without the translator, they could even use English like a secret decoder ring if Max turned off his computer translation program.

"My attendance is equality to Xander's attendance. The people of the Hidden People do not have cognitively immature youth."

"But the rest of the universe do," Max said. "They will dismiss Xander as unimportant."

"He is much very important!" Rick nearly bellowed.

Max whirled around to find a very curled up, angry ball of octopus near the foot of their bed. "Of course he is," Max assured Rick. Abandoning his packing, he sat near Rick and held his hand out. But Rick was having none of it. He kept all his appendages tightly curled. "He is exceptionally important, but the other peoples will think of Xander as a child. And even if they know the Hidden People are born cognitively developed, they will assume he has lived too short a time to do such complex work."

"They be pursuing tasks of greater complexity than I when similarly full of youth," Rick said. Some of the appendages twitched and seemed to straighten involuntarily. Yep. Rick was a proud papa, so proud he couldn't stay mad even when he wanted to.

"They are wonderful offspring," Max agreed. "We did good with them."

"We did." Rick's tentacles uncurled a little more. "All three offspring are important. However, Xander is small. However, Xander's smallness is significant in the lack of appropriate for assisting you in example of violence."

"You think I need better backup," Max summarized.

"Yes." Rick trumpeted the word loudly enough that it made Max's head ache.

Max stretched his hand out, and this time Rick wound his tentacle around it. "You lack eyes in logical rear position," Rick added. Max was tempted to make a joke about parents and eyes in the back of their heads in logical rear positions, but it was unkind to tease Rick when he was upset.

Rick lifted himself up and leaned into Max. "I dislike possible future where you do not return."

"I wouldn't do that to you," Max assured him. "I will always return to you."

"The thrill of victory and the agony of defeat are both always likely. Promise is only word." Rick's voice was softer now.

He had a point. Max had made the same promise to his mother, and he hadn't gone home to her even when he'd had the chance to. "I will always try to return. I fought through the Hunters to return to you and I will not let stupid people stop me from coming home."

Rick didn't answer, but he slid his tentacle under Max's shirt. The warm touch made Max smile. "Are you trying to seduce me?"

"Yes." Rick curled a tentacle around Max's leg and lifted it into the air, pushing Max onto his back.

Max laughed. "You are pushy."

"Yes," Rick agreed. Using his multiple appendages, he tugged at Max's pants and lifted him farther up the bed and teased a nipple all at once. Max captured the nearest tentacle and pulled it toward his mouth. He used his lips and tongue to explore all the small fingers on the underside of the tentacle. When he sucked it, Rick shivered with his whole body. As soon as he got control of his tentacles again, he flipped Max over onto his stomach and tugged his pants off in one motion.

"Bully," Max complained softly.

"You like me to positive connotation bully," Rick pointed out. Again with the logic, because Max really did. Rick ran a warm tentacle across Max's hole and all the tiny fingers teased the sensitive skin so that Max thrust down into the soft bedding. Rick took advantage of the moment and slipped the tip of a tentacle inside.

"No fair," Max said, "I want a tentacle up here." Max made grabby hands.

It drove Rick wild when Max sucked on the underside of a tentacle, and it was one of Max's favorite pastimes. However, this time Rick was not obliging. Rick gently pushed deeper in before he started the short thrusts he had learned to use to sexually torment Max. In and out, teasing with touch that wasn't quite enough. Max squirmed with need, but still Rick didn't change the too-gentle motion.

"You're killing me."

"Often you complain using hyperbole so I discount further death complaints."

"Hey, now."

Rick thrust his tentacle in so hard and so fast that Max yelped as the tentacles forced his body to adjust. He arched his back and gripped the edge of the mattress as lust caused a temporary white-out of all active brain cells. A few of the less important ones near the edge might have even leaked out of an ear. While Max was still trying to catch his breath, Rick slipped a second tentacle inside him. Max felt the tiny undulating fingers pulling at his rim.

"Careful," Max warned.

Rick crawled over Max's right leg before he settled on the small of Max's back. For a medium-sized octopus, he was a heavy bugger. "Always with you much care," Rick promised. The tentacles paused for a few seconds, and then the smaller one eased in and pulled out. Max's rim ached at the stretch, and he tried to spread his legs, but he was tangled with even more tentacles.

He moaned as he lost control of his body. He thrust down into the bed, and Rick bounced on his back as Max bucked. Then Rick did something with the first tentacle. He balled up the end or spread his tentacle fingers or something because Max was full and aching and gloriously well-fucked all at once.

"Fuck, yes."

"Yes, I am fucking," Rick agreed, and then he pistoned his tentacle in earnest. The smaller tentacle slammed into him while the larger one pressed deeper and deeper, filling Max until he squirmed helplessly, impaled on Rick's talented tentacles. "I am good fucking," Rick announced in the world's most dramatic bit of understatement ever. Max was losing his fucking mind, and he needed to come. Now. Before his last functional brain cell fell out of his head.

Rick pressed his tentacles deeper. The sensation was too much and too thick and not thick enough and just right and overwhelming and perfect and impossible all at once. Max wanted more, but the sharp edge of need threatened to cut through the lust-bliss he had going.

He reached for his cock, but two more tentacles tangled with his arm, pinning it down. Then Rick shifted up and a long tongue ran along Max's shoulder. With a scream, Max came all over their bed. His body twitched through the longest and most intense orgasm of his life. He was left limp and spent and still stuffed full of tentacle.

Max lay panting. It took several minutes before he could catch his breath, and in that time, Rick had shifted to one side, and he was playing with curling tentacles around and around Max's right arm and leg. "You didn't get me pregnant again, did you?" Max asked.

"No. Do you wish for implantation of offspring?" Rick asked.

Max pressed his forehead to the pillow. "Nope. No, three is enough for now. We still have to get them sorted and in good careers." Max didn't say it, but he also wanted to wait until he had the universe sorted. No children of his were going to get treated like trash. Nope. If Max had to shoot every prejudiced bastard in the universe one at a time, he would. He'd prefer to con them. And when the boys were ready to work, Max could front their inventions or they could find someone else to help. When the time came, they'd figure something out.

"If you wish the implantation of additional offspring, I am willing to implanting of additional offspring." Rick used a half dozen tentacles to trace circles on Max's body. Shivers of lust travelled like sparks under his skin, but Max's cock was worn out. Done. Finished. Spent. His cock might never work again, or at least not for a good hour.

Max smiled and rolled his head to one side. "I would be happy to have more offspring later. Much later."

"Clarify. Query. Later days, later weeks, later months, later years, later decades."

"Later months, maybe," Max said. Right now he had other thoughts on his mind, and he didn't want to be dealing with the universe while pregnant. "Query. Do you want more offspring sooner?"

"I wait for your approval of implantation of offspring."

"But what do you want?" Max asked.

Rick leaned his head against Max's shoulder. "I want Max large with offspring and unable to leave ship or confront others. I want Max to stay ship until he grows appropriate number of eyes to watch enemy. I want Max to remember pleasure to return to when he is talking to others of universe."

Max propped himself up on one elbow. "Did you fuck me because you're afraid I won't come back?" All the post-sex bliss evaporated like fog.

"Clarify. I give more reason to return after talking to others of others peoples. Happiest place not on Earth."

Max caught the nearest tentacle and brought it close enough for a kiss. All the fingers along the underside waved with pleasure. "If we never had sex again, I would return because I love you. We agreed to be boring together."

"Others peoples are less boring." Rick's tentacles kinked up.

"Our offspring keep me busy. I like being boring with you." That wasn't exactly what Max wanted to say, but he needed Rick to understand every word. "I love you. Sex or no sex, I love you. Other people like me or other people hate me, I love you. More offspring, no more offspring. I love you."

With each statement, Rick's tentacles began to relax, until finally several of his tentacles undulated in pleasure. "All your intestines turn symmetrical and digestive track rejects future offspring, I love you," Rick said.

That was the sweetest flattery Max had ever heard. Gross, but sweet.

Chapter Seven

Max stepped off the ship and looked around. Rick had parked in a sketchier part of the port. Maybe that was his choice to save money and maybe that was because the others wouldn't let him park his ship in the more popular areas. After all, they might get cooties. Max stopped at the bottom of the ramp and put his bag down so he could re-adjust his weapon.

Rick was all curly fries and stress about Max arming himself, but Max would not walk into this den of assholes unarmed. And he sure as hell wouldn't take his kids into a meeting without protection. The ship hatch *thunked*, and Max spotted Xander coming down the ramp. He had one tentacle around the controls of a motorized cart with the weapon prototypes and linguistic equipment. It was hard to believe he was the same age as the other two because Xander was tall enough that he could peek over the top of the cart. Weirdly, his head was smaller than any of the others. He was a lanky boy.

"Xander, are you ready for this?" Max asked. He was hyper-aware of the danger that others might overhear. So he kept his words vague and left the translator turned off.

"I am ready for much Max Father. However, I am very, very, very nervous. Query. I could make a mistake and reveal plans to enemies," Xander said in passable English.

Max took two fast steps up to Xander's side and whispered, "Let's not discuss this in public." Xander had inherited Rick's naiveté.

Xander widened a few of his smaller eyes. "Recording in public results in many violations of very many laws, and translation would require recording because others lack English database. However, I must repeat query. The probability exists where I commit a mistake and reveal plans to enemies." He seemed to have more confidence in others' ability to follow the law than Max did, but at least he had lowered his voice considerably.

"You have to specify whose enemies. They are, in this case, our enemies. Although they're not enemies as much as they are racist assholes who need to be taught a lesson." Max grimaced. He wished his kids were not on the wrong side of the universe's version of Jim Crow laws. Overcoming discrimination made for a hero story, but he had never wanted that for his kids.

"Racist assholes," Xander echoed.

Max walked down the ramp. "Don't swear."

"Your use of profanity is frequent," Xander said as he hurried after him. The cart whined as the sidewalk sloped up. Xander was playing Max's assistant, but Max itched to check on the cart. It was too large, even if Xander was taller than the average octopus.

Max kept his eyes forward. "Yes, but you're not supposed to understand English well enough to be able to imitate me."

Xander made a chirping sound that morphed into a whale song. When Max turned, two of Xander's tentacles were waving in the air, undulating with amusement. "Max Father is illogical. I am very, very, very good with language and very exceptionally excellent with English. Why would I not recognize words?"

Max blinked. "Did you ask a question without labeling it as a question beforehand? Good job." Max held out his hand and Xander gave him a miniature version of the high five. Max turned back toward the port city before any of the watchers could start questioning their relationship. Of course, if asked, Max would not lie about his relationship to any of the kids. That was the sort of damage that even expensive therapy couldn't undo.

Xander spoke louder now. "If I use interrogative word, I do not need to label question. I am still unsure how to identify a question with a lack of interrogative word."

"You know," Max said, "when that trader had his universal translation machine, the tone came through. I wonder if the difference between our translation computer and that big fancy expensive one is the computer's ability to identify tone. We should get translation samples from that machine and see if we can't figure out how to imitate it."

"The business communication facilitator is uncopyable."

"That's what other people want you to believe. People are quick to say impossible, but very few things actually are." Max had seen too many records broken and too many impossible feats accomplished before breakfast. Hell, he would have said an alien invasion was impossible, but then he'd gotten scooped up by invading aliens. Life liked irony.

"Why would people mislabel reality?" Xander, and all the kids, had an innocence that Max envied. They believed the world was fair, despite all the evidence to the contrary. Even James with his love of weapons design still had that childlike nature. For him, improved targeting was an academic problem, or at least he pretended it was. Max still worried that he had changed obsessions from ships to weapons after the pirate attack.

"In the case of the translation program, it might be so that they can protect their profit. Other times people want to believe things are impossible so they don't have to feel inadequate when they can't accomplish them."

"That assumes very, very much self-deception."

"Oh, hell yes." For a few minutes, Max focused on darting around a large group of Pajekh. The pith helmets were hard enough to hurt when one caught Max on the shin, and they had more tentacles than any one creature needed. They were navigational hazards on the sidewalk, and when they were in a group, they did not leave enough room for anyone else.

Max "accidentally" stepped on the smallest tentacle of one that pushed too close to Xander and the cart. Xander made a sound like a baby blowing a wet raspberry.

For a time, Max concentrated on making himself large enough to intimidate others out of his path so Xander had enough room for the cart. Max found that tentacle aliens were fairly nervous around stomping boots, so he made the most of his advantage. Eventually the sidewalk widened and Xander moved to Max's side.

"Why do you assume self-deception?" Xander asked.

Max glanced around to make sure no one was paying attention to them. "My people lie to themselves all the time. Don't you think your people lie to themselves?"

"Query. The last statement was a query?"

"Yes, it was."

Xander curled different tentacles around the cart's handle and rotated so his largest eye was pointed toward Max. "The Hidden People believe that to hide requires an individual to know where all one's individual tentacles are."

That was an interesting way to see the world, but Max wasn't so sure he believed it. "You've only met your father and brothers. How do you know what your people in general believe?"

"When Max Father is sleeping, Rick Father shows videos of Hidden Planet people."

So Rick was hiding videos of the home planet. That was curious. Max would have to poke that weirdness at some point. Maybe Rick thought he would freak out at the sight of too many tentacles, but Max had achieved "tentacles normal" status. "Maybe your people don't lie to themselves, but I think most people do." Max didn't have a lot of evidence for that, but he trusted his gut. Even during his encounter with the Hunters he had the feeling they were psychologically far more like humans than Rick's people were.

Xander didn't comment, which was probably a sign that he thought Max was stupid. Well, time would tell. If these aliens weren't as greedy and self-centered as humans, this con was not going to end well. If Max had learned one thing from *Leverage*, it was that the easiest mark was the asshole who was trying to con everyone else. You couldn't con an honest man.

Max led them through the arched entrance to the alleyway. He had thought he should go to the main door, but apparently the trader didn't want a moron human or his ugly assistant cluttering up the front of his shop. If Max hadn't needed this guy to make the con work, he would've loved to tell him to shove his head up his ass.

"Did you look at the files from the first meeting with the trader?" Max asked as he waited for a driverless delivery vehicle to pass them in the alley.

"Yes."

"Were you able to get the name of the trader from those files?" It annoyed Max that no one in this universe introduced themselves with a name. No doubt it said something about human culture that he needed a name when aliens didn't. After all, Rick had been willing to call the children Offspring One, Two and Three until the children themselves decided to keep the names that Max had chosen.

"The trader's name does not translate from his language. I can use the designation embedded within the recording to identify him for delivery of messages and packages."

They weren't far from the trader now, and Max started down the alley again. "Great. So we're going to have to resort to calling them Trader One, Trader Two, and Trader Three."

"If you choose an appropriate name, I can have the translation computer link the human name with the official designation within his own language," Xander offered.

Oh, that was so tempting. There were so many names that Max could assign this asshole. His sarcasm button itched. However, the aliens had managed to grab samples of earth languages during their little drive-by police chase. And Max couldn't afford to offend anyone that he might still need to manipulate.

So he needed something subtle. Nuanced.

He needed something that other people wouldn't recognize, but something that would let Max get enough sadistic pleasure that he could curb his urge to punch the asshole's oversized lips. Oh, there were so many possibilities. Max finally settled on his favorite. "Let's program his name as Al Bundy."

Xander blew a huge raspberry into the air, and little spittle spots appeared on the sidewalk underneath him.

"Don't you start," Max warned.

"Max Father is unkind." After a second, Xander added. "I like unkindness."

"You're more and more like your namesake every day," Max said. "But it's not technically unkind. It's sarcastic." He stopped in front of a familiar door. "This is it," he said. Then he turned his translator unit on before he touched the screen to request entrance. Cinnamon Carter from *Mission Impossible* had always looked so cool and collected when she was working undercover as a super-secret spy. But Max was fairly sure he was going to throw up. He hadn't been this nervous the day before his first solo flight. Come to think of it, he'd thrown up that morning, and right now he regretted not taking a detour down a less populated alley so he could privately vomit.

However, Al Bundy was opening the door, so it was too late for his Linda Blair impression.

Chapter Eight

Al Bundy led them up the back stairs without even glancing back to see if Xander needed help guiding the sample cart. He didn't, but Max resented that Bundy hadn't even checked. Asshole.

Instead of leading them toward the office where he'd talked to Max and Rick, Bundy turned in the opposite direction and headed deeper into the building. The hallway widened and the clutter vanished from the corners, so Max wasn't surprised when Bundy opened the door to reveal a room full of aliens. Pajekh and Chosen and People of Red, oh my. Max still thought it weird that the People of Red were sort of lavender-purpley, but he assumed "Red" referred to something less literal than skin color.

"This is quite the gathering." Max studied the gathering.

A Chosen slid forward. They were more humanoid than most aliens with an oversized upper lip and too many nostrils. If any species deserved to get called ugly, this one was up there. "Introduce person from undeveloped planet," it said in a wailing voice. The business communicator was on because the voice pitched up and down. However, since Max hadn't given Bundy access to the English database, the modulations were all translated into Hidden People whale song.

"That's me," Max said cheerfully. "Bundy, would you like to connect the English translator to the business communication facilitator? I brought the computer." He turned to get the equipment from the cart, and he heard several hisses and thumps behind him. Xander flinched back and his tentacles stiffened in a desperate attempt to avoid curling them. Only one thing would inspire that reaction, and Max didn't need a translation computer to figure it out.

Max whirled around. "Do not insult Xander." Max searched the crowd for someone to challenge him. He'd expected this. Every time he'd gone to a new base, he'd needed to prove himself to a room full of assholes who didn't trust him. Max had never backed down, and most of the time, those people had become his closest friends—the men and women he'd trusted at his back. He assumed any species that could become the dominant species of their planet would have a similar urge toward challenging each other. The aliens all stared back, silent and unmoving.

"Xander, plug in the English translation program," Max ordered.

"Yes, Max Father," Xander said. He came as close as any Hidden One could to whispering.

"It calls you father," the larger pith helmet Pajekh said.

That caused several tentacles to twitch, although none of them curled the way Rick's or the kids' did when they were upset. Either they weren't upset or they didn't have the same sort of physical reactions. Well if they weren't upset now, Max needed to make them worry a little. As long as they dismissed him as a moron, they wouldn't credit him with the ability to engineer anything, much less a complex navigational system. If they thought he was a bigger asshole than they were, he could pull this con off.

"He calls me father because I am his father." Max rested his hand on his weapon, and then his translator gave the distinctive chirp that meant it had connected to a new database.

"You were Ugly surrogate," a Chosen said, and the new translation computer was definitely working because the disgusted tone was unmistakable.

Max took a step toward the Chosen alien. "Among my people, someone who is a surrogate for a child or who adopts a child is considered a parent. Genetics does not define parenthood."

Bundy moved carefully between Max and the buyers. "Some species do accept parental roles outside of genetic lines, but I don't know of any species who accepts offspring of another species."

Max channeled his best Snidely Whiplash and sneered at the crowd. "I don't care what others do. Humans make their own rules."

The Tribes alien made a grunting noise. "Why would you accept responsibility for the Ugly One?"

"You are a bitch." Max mentally labeled this one Alexis Carrington, although part of that was the floppy hat. That was an eighties fashion statement if Max had ever seen one. "You had to go there, didn't you?"

"I state the obvious."

"Well then, here is an obvious fact for you. If I chop off an arm, you too will be asymmetrical. Asymmetrical is not a choice. And calling someone ugly because of a physical trait they cannot control shows how shallow and ideologically disgusting you are."

"Max Father." Xander touched Max's gun hand. "Do not anger buyers. Not for me."

Max smiled at his son. "If they insult you, they insult me." He turned his attention back to the room. Everyone watched him, and Max could practically read the thought bubbles over their heads. They were considering the possibility that they had completely misunderstood humans. Good.

"You should avoid certain emotional issues that could cause me to become upset," Max warned. "Children are one."

A Pajekh said, "Then we shall not discuss children of any state of ugliness."

"That would probably work out well for you since I imagine your children are exceptionally ugly," Max said. A pith helmet would not be stylish on any child.

"Max Father," Xander said in a horrified voice.

Apparently Max was doing a good job of upholding the Davis family tradition of humiliating children in public. Max's own father would've been proud to know that the torch had been passed, and Max was shouldering his responsibilities well.

"Are we done insulting each other? Can we get on with business, or does this ritual need to continue longer for you?" Max asked the room in general.

The Carrington alien answered. "I require clarification on the ritual you reference." Now that Max had named her Alexis Carrington, he was having a hard time thinking of the alien as anything other than a "she" even though he had no idea how the species understood sex or gender.

"I'm referencing this metaphorical pissing contest we're having. People on Earth quite often do this when they don't know each other, particularly when they believe they are in competition with one another. They push and threaten. They brag about their accomplishments, such as killing a whole group of Hunters while defending my ship and family, you know that sort of thing."

"Do you believe we would engage in Earth ceremony?" Carrington asked with unvarnished confusion. She was at least eight feet tall, so she peered down at him, her neck gill things flapping. The only other Tribes alien Max had seen had been his social worker, Heetayu, and that one had been even taller. Max was grateful there weren't more Tribes aliens around because it made him intensely uncomfortable to stand near an alien who was so much larger. However, he wasn't going to back down, especially not to someone wearing a yellow and fuchsia floppy hat.

"Sentient life comes with a territorial imperative and a need to defend what is theirs. Am I wrong?"

Carrington looked around at the gathered aliens as though expecting backup. The others watched her without offering a single word of support. She turned back to Max. "You adequately describe basic universal psychology. But there is no territory to claim here."

"Sure there is. Compensation is a form of territory. With more compensation, one may claim more ships and more land. Compensation is the core of territory. It is my desire to have a more stable territory with adequate fuel. That drives me to share my weapon design. My instinct says I should keep it to myself. After all, if no one else has my weapon, then I am unique and no one else can build a defense system against it."

"That is a violent way of seeing the world," one of the Pajekh said.

"I can be a violent man. I was chosen by my people as a defender. I was in a machine attempting to engage the Nish because of it. I was specifically chosen because of my accuracy in using weapons to kill others and I was trained to improve that skill."

Another Pajekh pulled all his tentacles up under his pith helmet like a hermit crab pulling all the vulnerable bits into the shell. That was a rather unambiguous sign of distress.

"But I would rather sell my inventions. Fighting is never my first choice," Max said before he freaked out the aliens any more. He wanted to be taken seriously, not to have everyone assume he was a psychopath. "But when I came to talk to Bundy here, I found out that you all assume that humans are morons, and that I was one more moron on the family tree."

"I have not said that," Carrington said. She drew up to her full eight feet and then did that neck fold trick to look him in the eye.

Max shrugged. "You're thinking it loudly." One alien twitched his tentacles and two more shrunk down the way Rick sometimes did when he was so upset the center tentacle curled. Maybe Max shouldn't have made jokes about telepathy. However, stress had broken his humor button back when he had first joined the Air Force, and the assholes that ruled the universe were not going to improve his ability to control his mouth.

"Humans are morons," an alien Max hadn't seen before said. He resembled a fringed purse, complete with two impossibly long "arms" that could pass for the handle. But Max had never seen anyone with bad enough taste to carry goose poop-green accessories. "They have not yet achieved space flight."

"Well, no. We haven't." Max had prepared an answer for this. "As near as I can figure, the dinosaurs were roaming the Earth when the rest of you found space. My people weren't even on the horizon. So considering that we started the race after the rest of you had finished and left that part of the galaxy, I don't think we're doing so bad. We have, after all, visited other planets in our solar system."

"Clarify dinosaurs," the purse demanded.

"The dominant life form on the planet when your ancestors were still in that part of the universe. They were all killed by a meteor strike that damaged the environment and killed all large lifeforms."

Carrington said, "Then the dinosaurs were the morons for not reaching space before the disaster. That is why reasonable species reach for outside their one planet. Accidents happen." She sounded very proud of that proclamation.

"Well, not really. You see, there had been three or four extinction level events that had already destroyed the environment before that. Our planet is a dangerous neighborhood." Max hadn't thought about it before, but knowing that life had to keep restarting did make him wonder why people hadn't panicked about having to reach space earlier. It shouldn't have taken a high-speed Nish pursuit to convince people that the planet was fragile.

Now aliens were looking at each other and tapping away on computer pads. Max had stirred them up.

"Now maybe we can discuss your complete inefficiency at developing weapons," Max said. "The wide scatter focus on the laser weapon that I confiscated off a certain Hunter that invaded my ship was completely inefficient. The targeting system is so inadequate that I couldn't fire from a distance at all, and even up close, it failed to adequately deliver the one thing I expect from a weapon—the ability to kill."

Oh yeah, Cinnamon Carter had nothing on him.

Chapter Nine

B undy waited until all the aliens had left before he said, "Humans might not be morons."

"That is probably true," Max said.

Xander made an amused burbling, but then he'd watched enough American television to know why Max felt the need to qualify that statement. After all, politicians were part of the human race, as much as Max would like to have denied that fact, and Max was not going to stand up for their collective intelligence. Officers assigned to Air Force One ended up more jaded than ones who served in active arenas.

Bundy continued. "The weapon design sold for more than anticipated."

"Yep." Max continued packing the cart. Xander handed him a prototype weapon to secure in the locking compartment. "The next thing I want to sell is the English translation database, but not until someone offers a ridiculous amount of money." The one time Max had walked into a department store in New York City he had learned the power of brand. If the store was a big name and the product had name-recognition, then people lost their ever-loving minds and paid hundreds or thousands of dollars on a pair of frickin' jeans. He needed people to put humanity in the same mental category as Tom Ford or Louis Vuitton.

"Clarify ridiculous," Bundy said.

Max didn't know if the word failed to translate or if Bundy was looking for a specific amount. He turned to face the alien. "Don't sell until a buyer gives you more money that you think is even reasonable. Then sell."

Bundy blurted, "I retain sixty percent."

"Oh hell no," Max snapped. "The translation program took much more time to create than the weapons. I know weapons, but having to work with words.... Oh, someone is going to pay me for that. You get twenty percent."

"Twenty is below standard!" Bundy's horror and anger came through his fancy translation program. Max hoped Xander was getting good samples to reverse engineer with their own translation program. Max had a fantasy of hearing the lust in Rick's voice when they tangled limbs. As much as Max knew the feeling was there, he wanted to hear it—not that he planned to admit that to his son.

"Fifty-seven," Bundy countered.

"Twenty."

"Fifty-five."

Max straightened and studied Bundy for a second. "Standard and not one percentage more. There are many traders who would work with me now. Carrington showed a lot of interest."

She had won the bid on the weapon plans, so clearly she thought there was profit in working with a human. Bundy drew his mouth up into an even more puckery pucker before agreeing. With that, he left, and Xander and Max were left alone to secure the cart before heading back to the ship.

"Max Father is brilliant," Xander said in English.

Max turned his translator off. "That was the easy part," he said. "I didn't make any claims that weren't true. The weapon design and the translation program are easy to pass off as mine because they are, more or less. James is better with the specific math, but I understand the theory behind all the changes we made. It's going to be harder to convince them I am capable of the sort of math your father does."

"They were full of fear. Very, very fearful."

"No, they were cautious and wary," Max said.

"Wary and fearful are functional synonyms," Xander said.

Max locked the last compartment and stood. "No, they aren't." He gathered his thoughts because he didn't want to teach Xander to use fear to get his way. Max hated bullies, and he wasn't going to raise one. "If they were afraid, they would run away from me. They didn't. They are wary because they are suddenly aware that I am dangerous."

"But if you pose a danger, would that not imply that their lives are in danger?" Xander asked.

"No. It implies that if they do something stupid to make me angry that their lives will be in danger, which is an excellent reason to avoid making me angry."

Xander didn't answer. With him, silence meant he was thinking hard. It was funny how different the children were. Kohei was quiet more often than not. He would occasionally ask questions and he loved to curl around Max's leg when he was telling stories or when they watched television, but he wasn't a talker. James, on the other hand, never stopped talking. It drove Rick nuts, although Max thought his enthusiasm was cute.

They guided the cart into the night air, and the winds whipped around them. "I think a storm is coming in."

Xander tucked himself down on the side of the cart protected from the wind, and Max moved to the back of the cart to shelter him. "Are you okay?" Max asked. Xander wasn't a child restricted to the water because of fragile skin, but Max still worried about him.

Xander wrapped a long tentacle around Max's wrist. "I am well." He triggered the rolling mechanism for the cart, and they rumbled toward the docks. The wind blew so hard that it whistled between the buildings and the raised walkways. Little whirlwinds danced through the pool of light cast by the strips that lined the undersides of what looked like gutters.

Max noticed that the streets were mostly empty, and he got the same creepy feeling he got during his short deployment to Bagram Airfield when it got too quiet. He wasn't superstitious enough to think it meant anything, but in Afghanistan, when it was quiet, he had time to think about the suicide bombers, the hatred and terrorism outside the secured perimeter. That probably explained why the servicemen and women spent so much time trying to keep busy.

But he had that same eerie feeling now as they walked through the empty streets. He had too much time to think about what he had said, and Max's stomach was tied in knots. This could all go so very, very bad.

Xander leaned closer. "You say you hoped to encourage their avoidance of your anger. Is that why you mentioned human affection for children?"

"Yeah. If any of those people hurt you, I would feel the need to hurt them back. They need to understand that danger."

Xander tightened his grip around Max's wrist. "The Hidden people retain privacy around their reactions."

"I think the word you want is secrecy," Max said, "Keeping secrets can be good. It means that people can't predict you well enough to counter your moves. However, sometimes people need to understand what you're capable of."

"So they can be wary of you," Xander finished. "Do you want them to fear you?"

Boy that was a loaded question. Max would rather be feared than treated like a moron, that was for sure. And the universe had put humans in that category. "No. I don't," he said, since that was mostly true. It was funny, but Rick never asked the sort of questions that forced Max to sort his thoughts. But children.... Children made his brain bend in directions that a brain wasn't meant to. "I don't want people to believe that I am so irrational that they have to be wary that my reaction will be violence when they haven't done anything to provoke violence. Do you understand?"

"Query. Do all humans feel the same?"

"No. I wish they did." There would be fewer wars if everyone had the same philosophy. "Some people like it when others are afraid." The opposite was also true. Max had known a few too many people in high school that hadn't been willing to warn their friends off any sort of bad behavior. Being popular was more important than being right. "Humans have much more variety in their reactions."

They reached the end of the shopping and residential district and as they left the buildings behind, the night grew darker and the wind stronger. Luckily the path had running lights or Max might have walked right off the damn edge. "Query. Is this subject related to bullying?" Xander asked.

"Where did you hear that term?"

"After school specials."

Those things had been the stuff of legend when Max was young—they were more his parents' generation. "Okay, I know no one is showing afterschool specials anymore. I haven't even seen them, and I've heard enough about them that I can safely say you should not use them to understand human behavior."

"I watched a documentary explanation of the function of afterschool specials. The function resembles educational videos shown by Rick Father."

Max doubted that. He was fairly sure they were more about wishful thinking and making kids conform, but then he'd never seen one, so what did he know. It did, however, make him worry about what else the kids might have seen when Rick had been grabbing signals Earth put into space.

Max didn't answer until he saw a figure near the tower that marked the beginning of the spaceship parking lot. "Hey look, there's your father." Max was about to call out a greeting when Rick turned and skedaddled back toward the ship. He paused. "Rick Father gets weirder every day," Max said.

"He is a good counterpart for Max Father." Xander blurbled with amusement.

"Dork." Max tried to turn on his translator and communication device, but Xander wouldn't move his damn tentacle.

"Rick Father hopes to quarantine any potential cooties," Xander explained.

Max stopped and pulled Xander around so they were face to sorta-face. "You and your father and your brothers do not have cooties. Now the rest of the universe, I'm fairly sure they do. You know how you were asking me about bullies? They are bullies. They have bully cooties."

Xander tilted his head. "They do not inspire fear. I can be in a room with them without wanting to run away."

"Really?" Max asked. "If I hadn't been there, would you have stayed in a room with all of those judgmental, rude people?"

"If Max Father had not been there, there would be no reason for me to be there." Xander had annoyingly perfect logic while still managing to miss the point.

"Query. Do you need compensation?"

"Currently, I do not. I am satisfied to remain with Rick Father and Max Father within immediate future. I would stay for when younger brothers appear."

Damn. That conversation took an unexpected turn rather quickly. Tabling the discussion of future children, Max returned to his main point. "Your father is afraid that he will not receive compensation for his work. They use fear to take something from him and better their own trading. That makes them bullies."

"In contrary, Rick Father accepts lower compensation that is natural. He has no fear, therefore they do not bully."

Max was seeing red so strongly that he had to take a deep breath before he yelled at his kid. He knew that Xander was being logical from a certain completely fucked-up point of view; however, he was not going to let his children accept an unfair universe. It was better to go down fighting than let bullies get away with bullying without a single protest.

"No, he only thinks it's natural," Max said. "They have bullied the Hidden People for so long that people accept the bullying. But that embargo on your home planet was intended to create fear and make the people change their behavior."

"They hoped fear of lack of compensation would make Hidden People unhide the Hidden Planet," Xander said.

"Exactly. So they are using fear, only there's this weird acceptance, and I don't accept anyone hurting my family."

"Which implies they are a threat and you feel justified in the use of violence," Xander said.

Max blew out a breath. He wasn't sure how Xander could be so right and so brilliantly wrong at the same time. "They are a threat to compensation, so I counter their threat with an attack on compensation."

Xander's tentacles waved. "I comprehend."

Max had learned that when it came to the children, or any pseudo-octopus members of the family, it was best to double check comprehension. "What do you comprehend?"

"Clarify. I comprehend Max Father fears his family will not receive compensation and respect. That means the others bully Max Father, and that is wrong. You should commit compensation violence against them." With that, Xander uncurled his tentacle and turned the speed up on the cart so it bounced down the walk toward the distant ship.

"That's not what I said," Max called, but Xander simply waved a few tentacles without slowing the cart.

Children. Max wondered if the human variety were as difficult to raise. If so, he owed his mother flowers and about a fuck-ton of good chocolate.

Chapter Ten

Rick was not waiting inside the door. Kohei and James were. Xander might have been the tallest brother, but Kohei was starting to develop thick tentacles.

The second Max closed the outer door to the ship, James was tangling around Max's legs. "Max Father. The compensation was much highly!" James sang happily. "Others like my weapons!"

"Of course they did." Max stepped over the clump of tentacles and excited offspring under his feet. "You make wonderful weapons. I've told you this."

"James's weapon changes are not James's alone," Kohei said. "Max Father gives idea."

"I work math!" James trumpeted.

"I able to math. Idea is more valuable," Kohei retorted.

Max felt as though he'd stepped back in time to a sibling fight between him and Petey, only now Max was playing the role of mother. "Hey, be nice to each other! Kohei, James has a right to be proud of his work. The weapon is his as much as mine, and he never said I didn't work with him." James drew himself up a little taller, so Max shook a finger at him. "And you, young sir, need to share credit. Not only did I work with you, but Xander is risking himself to help run this con, so you have to give him credit too. And I know you had him check your math several times."

James shrank back down, which inspired entire boat-loads of guilt. Parenting sucked. It was weird, but in the shows Max watched, the parents had to deal with slayer kids and werewolf kids and wizard kids, and those parents never seemed ready to pull their hair out. Well, usually not. Max was surprised he had any hair left, and that was on a normal day.

"We *all* did well today," Max finished. James slid away, and Xander ran after him, leaving Max alone with Kohei. Of all the children, Kohei was the one Max connected to least. Maybe it was because Kohei never needed him, not like his brothers. "Cut your brother some slack."

"He speaks rudely."

"We're family. If we can't be rude to each other, then who are we supposed to be rude to?"

Without a second of hesitation, Kohei said, "Buttfaces."

Sometimes the kids caught Max so off-guard that he didn't even have a response. Flying fighter jets required less concentration than parenting. The rules were more direct and the instruments were easier to read.

"If you're rude to buttfaces, they're rude back," Max said. "And sometimes that causes trouble that we don't want. Family loves us. They have to keep loving us no matter what. So when we're having a bad day, sometimes we take it out on family."

Kohei blew raspberries.

"Just don't assume the worst of your brothers."

Kohei glided silently away, and Max felt judged. Majorly judged. It dulled some of the pride he had about how the trade had gone, but on the good side, his fear that he was a shitty father mitigated any apprehension about the con.

Max headed deeper into the family section of the ship, the part Rick still wouldn't allow the children into. Rick wasn't waiting in the corridor either. Max headed up to their shared quarters, and even before the door opened, a rhythmic banging greeted him. His stomach knotted. It sounded like Rick was throwing everything they owned against the walls. Max hadn't seen that sort of anger out of Rick, and a little cowardly voice suggested he run for the hills. However, Max didn't run from fights. Well, except for that one time when his ex had thrown all his clothes off the apartment balcony, but Max called that a strategic retreat.

When he triggered the door to open, he braced himself for a shit-throwing fit and broken possessions. Instead Rick was braced on the edge of the bed with a mechanical panel open and he was pounding a piece into the back of it. He didn't even pause his work to announce, "I reviewed recordings. You are moron."

"I am *a* moron," Max corrected him, "and no, I am not." Maybe he shouldn't poke Rick's grammar, but that felt like a safer conversation than the one Rick wanted to have. Max sat on the edge of the bed, and Rick lowered the tool he'd been using and shifted so his eyes were on level with Max's.

"You lack logic."

"I can't argue with that," Max said with a shrug. His measuring stick for logic was Mr. Spock, and he fell so far short of that mark that it wasn't even funny. He couldn't even match a love-pollen-infected Spock for logic. No shame in that.

Rick tilted and then rotated to consider Max through multiple eyes. "Clarify your clarification."

Max grinned. Distraction level: master. Even now Rick's tentacles were relaxing. "My first statement is a correction of your grammar. My second statement is truth. I am not a moron."

"True and illogical is mutually exclusive and you are illogical."

"I am not."

"You am too."

"Am not."

"Am too," Rick shot back.

"Awww. Are we fighting?"

Rick froze. For a second he was like a giant stuffed octopus sitting on the bed. Only his eyes moved as they slowly rotated in their sockets. Then his tentacles all twitched. "Nausea, heartburn, indigestion, upset stomach, diarrhea!" Rick bugled.

"You watch too much television."

More tentacle twitching. "Television truths are still truths."

Max studied Rick. When they'd talked before, Rick had said he was fine with this plan, but something had changed. Max toed off his shoes and pulled his feet up under him. "Okay, tell me in small, simple words why you believe I am a moron."

"You are a moron." Rick sank onto the bed.

"So you say." Max sighed. "Clarify. Query. Why do you believe I am a moron?"

"Max presents self as violent." The smaller tentacles curled.

Max held a hand out, but Rick kept his tentacles to himself. "I can be." He kept his tone gentle.

"Nature of you not is violent. You could have given away my program to Hunters. You only are violent with Hunters when Hunters only say threat of violence against offspring." Rick trumpeted again.

Max was starting to think that Rick's grammar in his own language went to shit when he got upset. Either that or his accent got thicker or something because the computer struggled to get a coherent sentence out of Rick's more dramatic proclamations. "I see that you're upset," Max said slowly. He wasn't good at handling relationship conflicts. Hell, he wasn't even minimally competent at it; however, for Rick he had to try.

"You are moron," Rick said when Max took too long to finish his thought.

"Probably. I missed how much this would upset you, and I regret that."

Instead of soothing Rick, that made all his tentacles curl. "You planned threat of violence!" The voice was so loud that Max flinched away from the sound. *Damn.*

"I had to convince them I wasn't a moron."

"You are moron! You intent perception violence!"

Max caught Rick's tentacle and worked his fingers inside the tight curl. "They had a certain impression of what humans are like."

"Correct impression. Morons."

"Incorrect impression. Harmless. Helpless."

Rick's tentacle relaxed a tiny fraction. "The danger is that they will underestimate humans. You saw the television shows from Earth. You know the truth."

When he spoke, Rick's voice was as soft as Max had ever heard it. "Soap operas. Science fiction. Westerns."

It would be so easy to allow Rick to deceive himself, but Max didn't want to feel like a fraud, not with Rick. "News. Documentaries. War. Atrocities. Pol Pot. Hitler. Rwanda. Riots."

Rick's tentacles balled up again. "That humans are not Max human."

Max sighed. "No, and I hope I never see the sort of violence I've watched on the news, but I am trained to fight. My grandfather fought people who followed Hitler, and my family is proud of how many he killed. I'm proud of protecting my family against Hunters." Max swallowed a knot of fear and asked, "Are you frightened of me because I'm human?" Max couldn't blame Rick if he was. Television broadcasts of the chaos after the Nish invasion made humans look slightly psychotic.

"No fear." Rick flowed forward, his tentacles everywhere at once, and Max fell back onto the bed, and Rick's weight pinned him to the mattress. "I do fear nothing with you. I fear for you." The computer missed the next bit of whale song. "If others peoples believe humans are to be feared, they will treat you poorly. They hate Hunters almost as much as Uglies."

"Hidden people," Max corrected him. "I assume they hate Hunters in part because they hunt. I am not hunting. I am trading."

"Trading weapons," Rick said.

Max wished they had a copy of the trading translator and its ability to translate tone. Without knowing how Rick felt when saying that, Max was a bit in the dark. It was like trying to have a conversation through text—one where the other person didn't know how to use emojis. The tentacles helped, but there was a wide range of unhappy, and Max wasn't sure which variation was turning Rick into a side order of curly fries. "Trading weapons brings in resources," Max said softly. "James helped make those weapons and Xander helped me sell them. I am proud that we're working together to beat these assholes."

"I would prefer to hide."

Max spread his fingers and waited while Rick curled tentacles around them. "I will protect you."

"Who will protect Max?" Rick asked.

Max sighed. It was a serious question, especially when he didn't understand the psychology and legal system involved. Honestly, Max would have been more comfortable if he had someone on his six, and Xander didn't count. It was Max's job to protect him, not the other way around.

"Silly rabbit, Trix are for kids," Rick said.

"I have no idea what you mean by that," Max said.

Rick shifted around, and Max *umphed* when he caught a tentacle in the stomach. "Sorries." He settled next to Max on the bed. "Meaning. I am not made for providing helping. The Hidden people are best at hiding."

"Ah." Max got it now. Fear was a powerful motivator, and it might explain Rick's sudden desire to bang on the equipment. Max remembered when he'd gone home senior year and told his parents that he'd gotten an ROTC scholarship. His mother had lost all the color out of her face, and she'd been so scared that her little boy would get killed. Funny enough, back then alien abduction had not been on the list of rational fears. "My human family worried about me fighting, too."

"Extreme discomfort. They see you as violent—they prepare countermeasures with violence."

Max sighed. "I know that. I understand that violence is a double-edged sword."

"Violent individual uses sword, but sword is less worrisome than projectile and energy weapons."

Max laughed. "True." He stroked Rick's tentacle. "I will be more careful. I had to change their minds about humans. I had to convince them humans and harmless were not equivalent."

"Do not work too hard to accomplish that goal," Rick said. Max could imagine a fearful tone in those belches.

"Coming home to you will always be my first priority." Max traced circles on the back of Rick's largest tentacle.

"Perfect."

"But I would like to make the rest of the universe pay proper compensation, too," Max added.

Rick made loud farting noises. No doubt that was an editorial comment, but in this case ignorance was bliss. Max had no idea what it meant. And right now, he didn't care. He'd had a stressful day, and he had time to cuddle in bed with his Rick. That was all he cared about at this moment. He closed his eyes and let the stress of the day fade as he concentrated on the feel of smooth tentacles caressing his arm.

Chapter Eleven

Max was in the main corridor when Xander appeared with the equipment cart. "You ready?" Max called. Xander didn't answer, but James darted around the cart and came hurrying down the passage. "Max Father, I will go with you!" James announced loudly. The doors at the end opened again and both Rick and Kohei appeared. Apparently, they were having a family reunion.

"James is annoying," Xander blurted in English.

Max ignored the outburst. "I appreciate that James, but you need to stay here."

"No. I help Max Father." James stopped, forcing Xander to halt the cart. James was staging a sit-in. That seemed dangerous given how many tentacles he had and the weight of the cart Xander was controlling. It wasn't as if Xander was too small to retaliate anymore. Max knew he was going to regret letting them watch Earth television. It had crappy role models for sibling behavior.

Max looked helplessly toward Rick who hurried down the corridor. After a few seconds, Rick slid forward and curled a tentacle around James's torso. "Max Husband must work without offspring."

James shoved his father's tentacle away. "Untrue. Xander goes with Max Father."

"Xander has talent with language. Xander can assist."

James aimed his biggest eye at his brother. If octopus could've killed with a glare, Xander's days would have been numbered. James's tentacles were stiff as he said, "I can assist."

Rick moved closer to James. "I too wish to go with Max Husband. But my talent is programming, and I am not of help where Max Husband goes. Therefore, I logically stay."

"My talent is weapons. Cranky female-presenting creature requests help for weapons. Therefore, I go." With each word, James's voice grew louder. Substantially.

Rick leaned his torso toward Max, which he interpreted as a request for backup. Max moved to Rick's side. "Hey, kiddo. I wish you could go. In a fair universe, she would listen to your suggestions because you are very good at engineering. I bet you could do wonderful things if you came. But people aren't fair. The universe isn't fair. And if you came, she would not listen to you."

James's tentacles grew stiffer. Max had a flashback to Pete throwing a fit about Max's school camping trip where he had not been invited. Rick might talk about how offspring were born mature, but Max was fairly sure he was full of shit, because James was gearing up for a toddler temper tantrum.

"She ignores Xander," Max explained. "She is a rude poopy face with Xander."

Xander made bubbly noises of agreement. Max was lucky that Xander had less of a temper than James did or both, their potential client and James, would get an earful about how poopy they were being.

"She ignores Xander because Xander has talent with useless language. I have talent with weapons. With ships." After James made that proclamation, Xander grabbed at his brother's closest leg. James grabbed back. Before Max could do anything, Kohei had waded into the middle of the match and grabbed both brothers. He was so much stronger than Xander and James that he pulled them apart, and Rick caught James and held him to one side.

"Xander, take the cart out," Max said.

Xander spat at Kohei and said something untranslatable to James before he headed toward the door.

"I could help Max Father!" James said.

Max could imagine the wealth of frustration he would hear if they had the fancy business translator. And he got it. He did. As much as he hadn't wanted to be assigned to active combat, he remembered the frustration of watching other pilots get those positions. He'd railed against the unfairness of never getting the opportunity to prove himself, all because someone had spread a true rumor about his homosexuality where an Afghani translator overheard it. It sucked knowing that you weren't welcome, and it broke Max's heart that James felt shut out.

"You are brilliant," Max said as soon as Xander was safely out of the fray. Hopefully that meant James was listening.

"Much annoying with brilliance," Rick added.

Max grinned at him. "Yep, you make good offspring," he told Rick. The undulating tentacles suggested that Rick appreciated the compliment, even if James was still all stiff tentacles. "But kiddo, Carrington has this screwed-up idea that your people aren't worth trading with, just like she had a screwed-up idea that humans were useless and harmless."

"You taught her of screwing up perception with humans. Teach her different with Hidden People," James demanded.

"I am trying very hard to do exactly that," Max said. Having to look James in his eyes and tell him that the world was unfair—that sucked. Maybe if they could earn enough money, they could reveal the true author of the navigation program and then move to a part of space with absolutely no sentient life. Max was starting to think sentience was overrated. His family and a dog, and he'd be happy.

"Return to waters," Rick said.

"I'm not dry," James argued. He was sounding more like a toddler every second.

"Then go elsewhere." Rick's volume did imply snapping.

With more gentleness than Max expected, Kohei herded his little brother toward the door that led back into the main living areas. Max watched them go. "I hate this universe. *Star Trek* promised me that space was going to be better."

"Star lied," Rick said. "I didn't know I hated until you showed me reason for much hate. I am unsure whether you should say sorries or I should be grateful."

That was a pretty damn good summary of the whole fucked-up situation. "Maybe both."

"Logical and illogical." Rick blew bubbles. "Humans make life odd."

Max huffed. "That we do." He held a hand out toward Rick, and he curled a tentacle around it.

Rick didn't speak for several minutes. "I worry. Carrington is not with trustworthiness. Be very carefuls."

"I will," Max promised. "Trust me, I know all these people are backstabbers. They want profit, and they will hurt people to get it."

"They possibility hurt Max," Rick corrected him.

"I won't let them," Max promised.

Rick tightened his tentacle around Max's wrist. "Do not make with more violent words."

No one could do guilt like Rick. He was a master of the art. Max curled his fingers around Rick's tentacle and held on. He couldn't make promises, not when he wasn't sure how Carrington was going to treat him. Now that he had broken them out of the fallacy of believing humans harmless.

Rick headed after the kids. Feeling slightly worthless as a father and more stressed than ever, Max headed into the muggy morning air. This morning, the planet smelled of something sweet and earthy, like a strawberry that had gone off. Max sneezed, and Xander's tentacles flew up in the air.

"Max Father!" he bugled.

"It's a sneeze." Some days Max did not understand the family. They'd heard him sneeze dozens of times, and it never failed to freak them out. Apparently the idea of losing control over breathing ranked right up there with spiders and heights. Worse even. None of them could understand the fear of spiders at all, which had turned a night of watching *Big Ass Spider* into a week-long running joke about human illogic. Max never wanted to see a spider again, because then he would have four obnoxious family members pointing out the ridiculousness of being afraid of one. "I sneeze all the time." He headed down the empty boardwalk that led to town and the nicer part of the docks. Carrington had her ship in that section.

"Disturbing!" Xander said as he followed.

Max ignored the complaint. "I wish you would be more understanding with your brother."

"James is poop head."

"James is frustrated that he doesn't get to help. Look at it from his point of view—you get to help and he's left behind."

"Kohei and Rick Father are left behind."

"And he probably expects them to be equally frustrated."

"I never acted like poop head when you spent time with James. His work with weapons were of benefit, so I worked my project. I was not a poop head."

Max stopped and caught the cart to force Xander to stop, too. "Did I ignore you?"

Xander did a quarter turn. "Max Father spent most of his time with me when I was small. I was not small when Max Father worked with James."

That was definitely not an answer. "I spent too much time with James, didn't I?"

"You spent enough time to make James all, 'Marsha, Marsha, Marsha.'" Xander even raised his voice to mimic a girl's voice.

"Now you sound like Rick Father," Max said dryly.

"I sound more like Max Father, who loves human entertainment. My words are still truth. James is spoiled. Kohei never becomes poopy head." Xander started the cart moving again, leaving Max to stare at his retreating back.

Now Max felt worse. After a second, he ran to catch up. "I didn't mean to make any of you unhappy."

"James is unhappy because he is James," Xander said without an ounce of sympathy. "Max Father does not make offspring unhappy. He is like a brother in making me happy."

Max was almost sure that Xander was trying to say that Max spent lots of time teaching them, but that didn't assuage his guilt. "With humans, parents are supposed to treat children equally."

"Marsha, Marsha, Marsha," Xander repeated. "Humans have unreasonableness for parents."

Max snorted. "Asking parents to treat children equally isn't unreasonable. And I've hurt James, so I need you to be a little understanding." No wonder Kohei was being so supportive. As the offspring most likely to get ignored, he could probably sympathize. Max sucked at fatherhood. Sucked, sucked, sucked, sucked.

"Did your parenthoods always treat you and co-offspring equally?"

Max judged the length of the empty boardwalk between them and the ships in the posher end of the port. They had time, especially with the cart slowly bumping over the lines set in the walk. "My parents tried. I think my brother was frustrated because I got to do more than he did. He is six years younger, so it frustrated him that I got to go out on my bike and run around with friends when he had to stay with the babysitter."

"Did he torture the babysitter?" Xander asked.

"What? Of course not. Why would you ask that?"

"In entertainment, the offspring often torture the babysitter."

"Television isn't real." Max regretted letting them watch television. If they hadn't been hanging out on the edge of Earth space hijacking signals, Xander wouldn't have screwed-up ideas about humans. Actually, he would rather the kids not have accurate ideas about them either.

"Are families together the way entertainment shows?" Xander asked.

"What do you mean?"

"Do genetic relatives gather for celebrations and continue with alliances after reaching independence?"

"Yeah," Max said. "Of course we do." The second the words came out of his mouth, he realized that the question implied that the Hidden People didn't live like that. Xander was implying that he would grow up, move away and never come back. His breath caught and he stopped dead on the boardwalk. Xander continued for several feet before he stopped. Maybe something in Max's expression registered because Xander abandoned the cart and hurried back.

"Max Father. Identify wrongness."

The air burst out of Max's mouth and he didn't realize he'd been holding his breath. Xander curled tentacles around Max's wrist and tugged at him. "Max Father."

"I just realized you plan on leaving," Max said weakly. Fuck. No wonder Rick tried to keep his distance. The cute little bastards were going to break their fathers' hearts, or Max's anyway.

"Query. Do not human offspring leave? Query. Did not Max Father leave?"

Max sat in the middle of the boardwalk. The raised seam dug into his ass, but he didn't give a shit. After a second, Xander inched close enough to rest his leg tentacle against Max's knee. "I left, but I never meant to leave forever. Before the law-enforcement poop faces took me away from Earth, I called my parents every few weeks." Okay, that was almost true. Max hadn't called them often enough, but if six or eight or ten qualified as a "few," then he managed it every few weeks. "My mom was always asking if I had met anyone I wanted to pairbond with." When Max had failed at having any long-term relationship work, he'd started avoiding her. "But I planned to go home for either Thanksgiving or Christmas. I always visited home."

Max stared at Xander, wondering how he was supposed to react to the idea of losing his little boy. Intellectually he knew that Rick's people preferred novelty. Intellectually, he knew they weren't the most affectionate parents in the world. Emotionally, he was an idiot because he had never processed what steps one and two meant.

"Query. Identify wrongness," Xander said in a voice that was almost soft.

"I want you to be happy, but I don't want you to go away and never visit. I want to know your happiness. I want to meet anyone you feel is worth pairbonding with. I want to see your offspring. Shit. I'll never get to spoil grandbabies."

Xander rotated, catching Max's wrist with a new tentacle when he rotated too far to hold on.

Shaking his head, Max pushed himself up off the walk. "I can have a mental breakdown later. We have business to do."

"Max Father," Xander said, but Max had to focus. It was like when he was flying into difficult maneuvers—he had to focus on the horizon, on the instruments, on the feel of the engine vibration in the seat and the stick in his hand. He didn't have enough space in his brain to worry about anything else, so it all had to wait until after he'd landed the plane.

He strode down the walk, all his attention on the tall, black ship that Carrington owned. He tried very hard not to hear the *click-clack* of the cart behind him.

Chapter Twelve

Max touched the pedestal in front of Carrington's ship . The yellow glow shifted to a darker orange, and Max went to parade rest as he waited for someone to answer his call. Xander stopped behind him, and Max hoped he would remain silent. Max needed to concentrate on the enemy in front of him, not on his own personal dramas. It was a rule in the air that pilots forgot any conflicts and focused on the plane, the instruments, the act of flying itself. If a wife ran off or a kid was in the hospital, pilots drank and complained and emotionally fell apart on the ground—not in the air. Never in the air.

The door opened and a Tribes alien stood in the opening. It was so much smaller than the other two Max had seen that he wondered if it was fully grown. The creature raised its four-fingered hands in a strange yoga-looking pose before coming down the ramp.

"Leader of ship Tribe within," it said.

Max glanced at Xander, but he didn't appear alarmed at anything the alien said. When Max had to rely on a child a few months old for intelligence, he hadn't prepared well for the mission. But in his defense, human-to-anything except Hidden language pretty much sucked without the fancy business translator.

"Lead away," Max said. Oversized eyes blinked at him, and the neck gill flaps fluttered before the alien turned and headed into the ship.

"Max Father weird," Xander said softly.

"You don't know the half of it," Max muttered before he followed the Tribes alien. Max was halfway up the ramp when the wall of humidity hit him. He felt as if he'd been dropped in the Deep South in the middle of summer, and not the literary version of the South with magnolia trees and wide verandas, but the real one with sweat stinging his eyes and doorknobs that burned off a person's fingerprints. A bead of sweat rolled down Max's spine and he scratched it. "Are you okay?" Max asked Xander.

"Uncomfortable but healthy," Xander said.

With a nod, Max headed into the ship's interior. The light was bluish and uneven and the air even more humid as he stopped in the central corridor. A familiar computer display blinked for attention, and Xander moved to the controls and hooked up their computer. The business translator flashed.

"Are we connected?" Max asked. He disliked giving Carrington access to the English database, but Bundy and Rick both insisted that the business translator's internal security would prevent pirating. And since Max trusted one of the two, he had to take the chance.

"Done," Xander said.

Max looked toward the end of the corridor, but his short guide had vanished. A Tribes alien stood near a door. This one was closer in height to Carrington, but the wide-brimmed eighties hat was missing, which made it hard to tell. Without the hat, the illusion of gender vanished, and Max had to consciously avoid staring at the weirdly proportioned arms with their long forearm at the end of a very short humerus.

"Hello." Max started down the hall, his boots echoing against the metal decking. The plates were solid instead of the grating he had grown used to on their ship. "Are you the trader I met yesterday?"

Neck gills fluttered. "Would it be customary to offer welcome to my ship?" She crossed her freakish forearms across her chest.

"A greeting of some sort is usual for humans. Good morning."

Carrington uncrossed her arms. "What an interesting expression." Her voice sounded curious, so the business translator was on. Max wondered if she had it hooked to her ship's main computer or if her wrist communicator had a connection. It would be awesome to have a system that always worked on their ship. Sometimes after sex Rick got very chatty, but if he didn't remember to put his communicator back on, Max missed most of the words. After Max had bashed his wrist communicator against the headboard once, he'd banned his translator from bed. They couldn't afford to replace it too often. Carrington continued. "If you do not like someone, do you recommend they have a less than good morning?"

"Sometimes," Max admitted. "Most of the time, we ignore them, or we say good morning anyway to avoid conflict."

"Avoidance of conflict is a positive social trait. I am gratified to hear humans possess such a behavioral imperative." She studied Xander, and Max's temper frayed. Maybe she hadn't meant to imply that his love for Xander was a less gratifying behavior imperative, but Max was a hair breadth away from unloading all his frustrations on her, and he had a lot since his conversation on the boardwalk.

"Humans also have a behavior imperative to protect their children," Max warned.

She made a clicking noise. "I have no difficulty accepting your fondness for the asymmetrical ones."

That felt too similar to calling Rick's people ugly, but at least it was a factual version of an insult. Max chose to ignore it and focus on the job. "So what concerns you about your defenses?"

"Many things," she said vaguely. "What convinced you to work with Bundy? He is a questionable choice of partner to broker compensation for your efforts."

"I thought you traded with him," Max said. He had expected Carrington to fish for information, but naively he'd thought she would be more subtle. Instead, she was approaching the topic of Max's motives with all the grace of a drunk elephant.

"I trade. I do not trust." Carrington turned and headed farther into the ship. "Come. Leave the equipment here, and it will be left unmolested."

That was an interesting verb. Xander was already locking the wheels. Max waited so Xander could come with them. He wasn't going to leave his son in the middle of hostile territory, that was for sure. Max only followed Carrington once he made sure Xander was coming. "I don't trust either him or you."

"A wise choice," Carrington said without turning. The light was shifting toward more green tones and getting darker. "Do you avoid any answer to my question by intent or accident of verbal ordering?"

Max had wanted to avoid the question of his relationship with Bundy since it wasn't exactly legitimate, but nothing communicated guilt faster than evasion. As someone who was guilty, Max would've liked to avoid the appearance of it. "I chose him because he had tried to get a license to trade on the Hidden World. He was turned down."

"So his lack of trustworthiness from the perspective of the Ugly Ones led you to trust. An interesting logic."

Max reined in his aggravation. "I assumed if he would trade with the Hidden People that he would trade with me. After all, I understand the government computers listed me as a moron."

Carrington turned. "Humanity in general. No doubt they did not judge you personally."

"Considering that the universe has almost no experience with humans, I assume that judgement is based largely on the observations of me when I was suffering from panic and confusion," Max said. Thinking back to his time on the police ship, he was man enough to admit that he'd been a whiny, panicked, annoying baby. "My people assumed aliens existed somewhere, but I did not expect a ship of aliens to take me off my planet."

Sure, there were people who assumed exactly that, but generally they didn't pass the psych eval to become an Air Force pilot.

"So you trusted Bundy's lack of judgment when seeking trading partners. That does have merit. I notice the translator has assigned the verbalism 'Bundy' to the trader, but the computer offers no translation of such mouth noises."

Since Carrington hadn't asked a question, Max ignored the comment. "When we were boarded by Hunters, the ship had no internal sensors to warn us. Do you have internal alarms?"

She turned so fast that Max nearly lost his balance trying to brake fast enough to avoid running into her back. "Why would we require internal alarms? Do not external alarms provide more effective defenses?"

"Assuming they work," Max said.

"Would not a captain immediately land a ship with defective proximity alarms?" Carrington asked, her voice higher and faster now. Tribes aliens were the only ones who had any passing resemblance to humans, so Max's brain told him that meant she was panicking, but his common sense warned him not to apply human assumptions.

"If I were a Hunter, I would do something to trigger your proximity alarms over and over, particularly at a time when you were not near a place to land."

"And how would that provide you access to my ship?"

Max smiled. "I don't know your people well, but is it possible that an individual might get so tired of having to check a seemingly faulty alarm that he might turn the alarm off?" Max didn't know if that was what the Hunters had done to Rick or if Rick's ship had malfunctioned so the alarm sounded often enough to annoy Rick into deactivating it. Their translator wasn't nuanced enough to ask, and Max wasn't sure he wanted the answer.

"An individual would have to suffer a lack of logic to make such a mistake," Carrington said.

Max didn't say it, but he agreed. Rick was brilliant, but not necessarily smart. "And would any of your crew be tempted to turn off an alarm if it annoyed them?"

Carrington didn't answer for a long time. Eventually, she turned her back on him and started walking. "Would the installation of internal alarms negate the danger?"

"Possibly. I would like to look at the ship's schematics to consider weak points in your security. If I get a sense of where someone might want to breach your ship, we can work on sensors. And who would be responsible for security inside the ship? Do your people fight or hire fighters for your ship?"

"Your people think like Hunters," Carrington said.

"I'm not sure if I should be offended."

She turned. "You should only take offense if I describe you inaccurately."

"I am trained to hunt." That was a slight distortion since hunting people was generally off limits, but he hunted targets in his jet, so close enough. "However, it is not in the nature of my people to steal. Many of my people will steal, but the rest of us consider that unacceptable behavior and we will punish it."

She studied him. "The initial assessment of human nature was critically flawed."

"Yes, it was. So, do you want a security assessment of your ship, or did you invite me here because you hoped to do your own assessment of my nature?"

"I purchased your weapon design. Does that not imply my respect for judgment?"

"You haven't answered my question about whether your ship has fighters on it," Max said. "If you don't give me information, I can't assess your security." Max looked at Xander. "I get the feeling she doesn't trust us."

Xander made a spitty sound, which usually meant amusement, but his tentacles were a little stiff and jerky. Max wasn't sure how to read that.

"You ask for sensitive information," Carrington said.

"You asked me to assess your security."

Her neck gills fluttered.

"And this ship is not comfortable for me. It's far too warm and there is too much humidity in the air, so it makes me cranky."

"Cranky Max Father says things he regrets later," Xander said.

Max laughed. "That I do, kiddo. So, what do you say?" he asked Carrington. "If you want me to assess your security, I can. If you wanted a chance to talk to me privately and see if I was as stupid as the government computer said, then I'm happy to leave. No charge."

The silence went on so long that at least three sweat drops rolled down Max's spine. "I will introduce you to Tribes fighter," Carrington said. "You can talk to her about new weapon design and internal security."

"That sounds like a deal." Relief washed through Max, but so did a sense of direction and purpose. Sure, Rick and the kids saw him as a warrior, but the rest of the universe had taken the darkest point of Max's life and judged him on it. They'd labeled him an idiot because he'd had too many moments of flailing panic.

He hated when others looked at him and decided they knew who he was based on some piece of information. When his commander in Afghanistan had pulled him in to talk about the inappropriateness of Max flaunting his sexuality in the Middle East, Max had tried to defend himself, but Colonel Barrington had made up his mind. To that old dinosaur, gay meant flouncy and queeny and flamboyant, and he didn't want to hear anything that might contradict his dumbass assumptions.

And that was exactly what the universe had done. They had decided humans were odd, panicky, stupid creatures and nothing Max said convinced them otherwise. Until now. Now they were seeing the real him. Capable. A little dangerous. Still weird. Yeah, Max could own that one. He was definitely a little odd.

Chapter Thirteen

Max sighed as the door slid closed behind them. Home. He had never been so happy to see the inside of his little ship. Rick came out of a side room. "You return in sighing," he said.

Max watched Rick's tentacles get wavier and floppier as he closed the distance between them. he caught a tentacle in his hand. "Carrington is sending payment over. We helped her people plan for a potential breach attack."

"Father Max impressed with violence," Xander said.

Max cringed as Rick's tentacles stiffened. "Snitch," Max muttered before he turned his attention to his unhappy husband. "I was not violent to Carrington's people. I was perfectly polite."

"Xander says impressed with violence!" Rick protested with a trumpet.

"I impressed them with my theoretical violence against invading peoples. I was not violent."

Xander blew raspberries while Rick did a little quarter turn. Ignoring the little shit, Max pulled Rick closer. "I was very non-violent. You would have been proud of me." That was even true if Max ignored the way he had horrified Carrington's head of security with a detailed description of how to use a maintenance hook to disembowel the enemy. That had not secured his reputation as a sane, nonviolent individual, but if Hunters did get on the ship, Carrington's people were now prepared.

Eager to change the subject, Max turned his attention to Xander. "I noticed Carrington was using female pronouns for you. Have I been wrong about your gender?" Guilt gnawed at the idea that he'd spent months calling a girl by a boy name and he couldn't even tell the difference. Then again, Rick had demonstrated his genital tentacles and they still looked like the tool manipulation tentacles which did not appear different than the foot tentacles. And, for that matter, Rick tended to use all of the above equally well when having sex. So boy versus girl was still a mystery when it came to Hidden people.

"I do not wish to be female," Xander said. "I do not prefer to spend time on appearance."

"Whoa!" Max blurted. "Female does not mean spending time on appearance. Where did you even get that?"

"Television," Xander said.

Max had a flashback to his mother complaining that the "boob tube" was a bad influence on the kids. His father had never done more than grunt unless she got shrill. Then their father would drive them outside to get some healthy air. Their childhood home had been a half mile downwind of a cattle farm. He would not have described the air as healthy.

"All females I observed on television are more decorated. Buffy often moans over the loss of shoes. I do not have time for decoration on my face."

"You mean they wear more makeup? Women don't have to wear makeup."

"Okay," Xander said, and then he started pushing the utility cart down the hallway.

"Wait," Max called, unwilling to let this misunderstanding stand. Xander ignored him and headed through the door into the main junction. "It's not like that," Max said weakly.

Rick tightened his tentacle around Max's wrist.

Max sighed. Kids. "It isn't like that. So, how is James?"

"Equally unreasonable." Rick slid closer. "Query. Define difference male or female."

"Males produce sperm and females eggs." Max frowned. Wait. That wasn't true. "Most females produce eggs and some don't produce anything. And males are still males if they can't make sperm. Sometimes men get cancer or things happen, although most men avoid talking about it. And there are a few women who produce sperm. That's a little less common."

Rick did a quarter turn, hesitated, and then quarter turned again. Yeah, he could consider Max with every eye he owned, and that still wasn't going to make a lot of sense. "It's complicated," Max finished. And the older Max got, the less he understood. "What do you think the differences are between male and female?"

"Females have less hair," Rick said with confidence. Max blinked as he processed that. Unexpected and yet more accurate than Max's attempts to clarify the issue. Rick must have assumed the answer was incomplete because he added, "Although apparently many women attempt to compensate for lacking hair with the growing of more longer with limited hair available."

"They have hair that they choose to shave off because they like hairless bodies."

"Query? Clarify."

"Why women shave? I have no idea. I don't know a lot about women. That's part of being a gay man."

"Query. Qualifications of being man."

Max was far too tired for this conversation. He headed toward the family living quarters, Rick holding his hand and walking beside him the whole way.

"Max. Clarify qualifications."

Max's first instinct was to point out that he had a penis, but then he would be right back to that gray area around transgender. As a gay man, Max tried very hard not to disrespect other people's sexes or genders or sexuality, but the minute he took penis and vagina out of the equation, he wasn't sure how to define man. He must've hesitated too long because Rick tugged him to a stop.

"Observation from television. Query. Males are more aggressive?"

That was a loaded question. Max knew the testosterone did tend to ramp up aggression or aggression ramped up testosterone. He wasn't sure which was which. But he also knew that there were plenty of women who had tempers that could level entire buildings. Ditzy Dee had been an aggressive pilot, and there had been a captain... oh God, what had been her name? Something horribly normal like Clark or Smith or Jones. But everyone called her Captain St. Helens. She didn't need a penis or male levels of testosterone to be aggressive. "I don't think it's that simple. Gender and sex and hormones and social rules all get tangled up. I think males act more aggressive because women who are aggressive... that's not seen in a good light by my people."

"Like Buffy."

"What?" Max had missed a conversation turn or two because he was lost.

"Buffy Summers burned down the library, but authorities failed to query existence of vampires before blaming." Rick tugged Max into motion, guiding them down the hall. "They should have queried, but aggressive women are not queried."

"You're absolutely right," Max said. "You do realize vampires aren't real, right?"

"Construct of fear, but within fictional universe fictional vampires as nonfictional as fictional Buffy."

Sadly, Max had followed that train of thought. "You're probably right. The show Buffy tries to be feminist, but sometimes it proves what a sexist world we live in. On the other side, violent Faith is kinda hot. She almost makes me want to give girls a try."

"Query. You find violence attractive?"

"No. No, that is not what I meant. I'm into fictional violence." That still sounded bad. "I like people who stand up for themselves."

"Query. Why share preference for Faith violence?"

"Good question," Max muttered. Rick always did get him verbally tangled enough that he said something stupid. Since he couldn't explain his joke about violent women, he went back to Rick's original question. "Gender is hard to explain, because some of it is what people expect and some of it is the biology, and it's hard to tell how those two things work together. But, women can be fighters as much as men. One of the pilots who died when the Nish invaded my planet was named Dee. She was one hell of a fighter. She might've been a better pilot than me, not that I ever would've admitted it."

Max remembered watching the alien fighter line up on her tail. He'd called out a warning to her, but he didn't know what happened. He had a flash of a memory—a fighter exploding in a shower of sparks, but he couldn't remember whether he'd seen her blown out of the air or if he was taking the memory of seeing Dan's jet destroyed and superimposing it over the memory of Ditzy Dee.

"Max." Rick moved to block the corridor and a half dozen tentacles came up to encircle Max. "Clarify. Sweat turns ugly scent."

"You sniff me?" Max was mildly horrified. Okay, so maybe he loved the smell of a sweating man, but he generally didn't announce that to the world.

"Sniff requires nose. Hidden People taste. You scent taste of ugly. Clarify." Rick tangled his tentacles around Max's legs so he couldn't go anywhere, even if he wanted to.

"I'm tired after dealing with Carrington. Maybe we can talk about this later." He smiled at Rick.

"Later scent is gone. Query. Carrington caused ugly scent." Rick was upset enough that he trumpeted out a string of untranslatable words that Max assumed were profanities. He had an image of Rick, all outraged, stiff tentacles taking a swing at Carrington. It wouldn't end well.

Max wrapped his fingers around the closest tentacles. "Hey, this has nothing to do with her. I am remembering the people who died because the Nish tried to dodge around a tiny planet in an unused corner of the galaxy to escape capture. It's just all so stupid, and good people died because of that stupidity."

"Earth is perfectly normal-sized." Rick had a solemnity that made Max snort laughter so hard that he hurt his nose. He felt as if he'd snorted pool water, and Rick hadn't even said anything funny. Rick tightened his tentacles.

"I miss those guys. Dan-Dan was a shy guy. The nicknames we used, we did this weird opposite thing, so we called him Dan-Dan the man. He couldn't talk to girls without forgetting his own name, so how he got a woman to marry him... none of us understood. He had a two-year-old girl at home. He had punched out of his jet when a Nish ship tore through his parachute." Max closed his eyes as his mouth tried to twist into ugly shapes. He fought back the urge to cry. "And Ditzy Dee—she was a damn good pilot. Always had her nose in a book." Rage washed through, erasing the pain. The fucking Nish and the fucking police chasing them. Good people had died because they hadn't cared about the people of Earth.

The whole universe was full of assholes who never considered other points of view. Giant fucking assholes.

Rick tugged on Max's arm. "What inappropriate nickname did they call you?" Rick asked.

Again, an involuntary snort of laughter escaped Max. "Mad Max," he admitted.

Rick and the kids had seen the movie, and Rick probably considered it more appropriate than the guys back on Earth had. They'd seen him as quiet, polite—on the masculine side of effeminate, but not by much. He remembered Dan asking him where to get a custom tux and a male manicure. He'd assumed Max would know. At the time Max had assumed the guy was being an asshole and stereotyping the only semi-open gay guy in the unit. Now... now Max regretted every second he lost not appreciating the people he'd had in his life.

Max didn't have the vocabulary to explain any of that. "They saw me as kind and a bit soft," Max explained. "I trained to kill, but I was not the sort of man who wanted to kill. I still don't want to kill, but I will. But the fact that I am less violent does not mean I am less male."

"Humans weird."

"I can't argue with you there, buddy."

Rick pulled him closer, pressing their bodies together. Rick was smaller, but Max still leaned into him. For a short octopus, he was sturdy because he held Max's weight and even tightened his hold. They stood leaning into each other for a long time before Max started pulling back, struggling to get his balance—physically and emotionally.

"Query. Do you consider me male or female or neither or both?" Rick asked.

Max was relieved at the change of topic. "I guess I consider you male."

"Query. Reason."

Shaking free of Rick's tentacles, Max looked around. They were outside the door that led to the private quarters. "I suppose because I'm sexually attracted to males and I am sexually attracted to you. Therefore, I see you as male," Max opened the door and headed into the soothing colors of the family section of the ship. "I think some of that also has to do with your inability to carry young."

Rick blew raspberries, and Max turned to poke a finger in his direction.

"Let me be very clear. That does not make me female. Nope. Not even a little. Don't go there."

"None of my species has capacity to carry eggs of young."

"Then I would think of your entire species as a planet of males." Males with very talented tentacles, which would inspire a whole lot of porn if people on Earth ever found out. "Query. Do you see yourself as male or female?" Max asked. It only now occurred to him that he had never asked the question before. If Rick saw himself as female, Max would have to deal with being a little less gay, but it wouldn't change their relationship.

"I am unclear how human definition and sex interacts."

"Oh trust me, you are an expert in interacting sex parts." Max waggled his eyebrows. "In case you didn't catch it that was me complimenting you on your ability to have sex." This was a far happier conversation, and Max threw himself into the innuendo. If he could get Rick interested in some tentacle sex that would be even better.

"Max weird." Rick caught Max around the waist and shoved him against the door. The door slid open, and they fell into the elevator in a tangle of limbs and tentacles. Max laughed, and Rick blew raspberries, and for a time, Max pushed all the big questions aside. He had a husband and some privacy and time before he had to get back to his con, and that was as good as it got. Max certainly didn't need any more than that.

Chapter Fourteen

Max led the way through the public areas of the ship and into the more decorated inner sanctum. "Are you ever going to invite the kids into this part of the ship?" Max asked.

"When offspring no annoy," Rick said loudly.

Given James's ability to drive his father up a wall that might take a while. Even Xander tended to pester Rick when he wanted something. Max might have been able to talk Rick around when it came to Kohei, but that would make the other two resent their brother, and Max wouldn't do that. He wanted the kids to like each other.

They approached their private quarters, and Max stretched. "I am so tired." Dealing with Carrington stressed him out.

"Query. Max avoid tangling tentacles from tiredness?"

Max stopped and caught the closest tentacles so he could pull Rick closer. "I am not too tired for tentacles. I am never too tired for your tentacles."

Rick shimmied.

"I am too tired to deal with Carrington," Max added.

Rick's tentacles curled up tight. Max sighed. He should have known better than to bring up Carrington or the con in general. Rick was not on board with demanding fairness from the universe. He tugged Rick toward their bedroom. "I could be on the verge of passing out, and the promise of your tentacles would wake me up." Max triggered the bedroom door. He backed into the room, pulling Rick along with him.

Rick curled his tentacles around Max's arms, pushing at his clothing and caressing the newly exposed skin. It was arousing as hell, but then Rick could belch and Max found it hot. "Don't rip my shirt."

Max went to pull his clothes off, and for a second, Rick held onto him, tentacles curling around him and holding him captive. Then with a blurble, Rick released Max.

"Clothing inconvenient," he complained.

"I get cold far too easily to give up clothes," Max said. Besides, the rest of the alien species preferred clothing, some of them had quite extravagant clothes. Running around naked when the rest of the universe was wearing clothing felt far too risqué for Max's taste. Max was a little impressed that Rick was so unconcerned about what other people thought of his unclothed tentacles.

The door closed once Rick had all his limbs inside the room. While Max had his hands over his head to strip off his shirt, Rick slid closer. He ran his tentacles up Max's bare chest and around the back of his neck. Other tentacles slid under Max's pants so the waist band became tight with all the squirming tentacles pushing inside.

"Wait," Max gasped, distracted by fingers questing down his crack. "Let me get the button."

Rick brushed the tip of a tentacle across Max's lips, those talented fingers along the underside of it teasing with feather-light touches.

"Fuck," Max whispered. His fingers fumbled as he tried to open his pants.

"Fuck," Rick echoed softly, and then the tentacle slipped inside Max's mouth.

Max gasped, and then Rick rubbed his collarbone before more tentacles wrapped around Max, undulating and twitching as Rick pushed him back toward the bed. Max found that sucking on the tentacle, unfastening his pants and walking backward was a combination he hadn't mastered.

He lost his balance and stumbled. Rick tightened all his tentacles so that Max was caught, supported by about a dozen tentacles at once. Rick was strong, but he rarely showed that strength. But he had no trouble lifting Max to the bed.

Max shoved his pants over his ass before Rick could do his rip-and-tear routine. He had a thing against clothing. Rick took the opportunity to shove the pants to the floor, and then Max's underwear followed, leaving soft, cool tentacles pressed against Max's hot skin.

Knowing what Rick wanted, Max curled his arm around the closest tentacle before tickling the spot where the underside met Rick's body. That made all Rick's finger tentacles wiggle in pleasure. Yep, Max knew his octopus. He grinned as the tentacles around him shivered and undulated.

Rick curled a tentacle around Max's thigh, pulling his legs apart so Max's hole was obscenely exposed. "You are a naughty octopus," Max said.

"Max like naughty." Rick had a two-toned belch.

He wasn't wrong. Rick pressed against Max's hole, and Max moaned. A hundred touches all demanded his attention at once. Max breathed harder as his skin grew more and more sensitive. Fingers danced over his shoulders and his nipples and the backs of his knees, and Max's brain couldn't keep up with the way his whole body hungered for more.

That called for a counterattack. Max pulled on a tentacle, exposing the "underarm" area, which was a prime tickle target. Max ran his fingertips over the sensitive skin, and Rick shivered. However, a questing tentacle ran across Max's pebbled nipple, the fingers teasing and tugging at it as the tentacle curled around.

Max's cock twitched and heat gathered in his balls. At one point he hadn't liked the idea of tentacles in his bed. He'd been an idiot. Rick was a sexual god. "I missed you today." Max ran his hands up those well-muscled tentacles. "I've gotten used to spending all day with you."

"Max stay inside. I am happy," Rick said. Even without proper grammar, he was very easy to understand. But as much as Max wanted to make Rick happy, he didn't want to give the rest of the universe carte blanche to disrespect his family. He had to get them to see Rick the way he did—as a gentle genius—a shy creature who had an endless capacity for love.

Rick tightened the tentacle around the base of Max's cock. Max's body arched and his breath grew quicker. Rick had such an advantage with all those tentacles and hundreds of fingers, all of which could tease and torment at once. Apparently in addition to being a gentle giant, he was a little bit of a sadist. Just a tiny bit.

That feeling was reinforced when Rick's fingers pulled at Max's nipples and teased the slit of his cock at the same time. Max's whole body was hot enough for spontaneous combustion. Max couldn't control his reactions when Rick got his tentacles going. A tip pressed against Max's hole, and he gasped.

"You..." Max grunted as the tentacle eased in.

"Me," Rick said with confidence. He entered Max with a single, strong thrust that stole Max's breath. White dots floated through Max's vision as Rick pressed against his prostate. Throwing his head back, Max sucked in a hungry breath as he trembled.

Rick rumbled, his voice a vibration more than words, or at least the translator didn't offer any specific translations. Max squirmed, ramming his hips into the air to take the pressure off his ass, but Rick took the opportunity to drive farther into Max.

Soft touches teased the inside of Max's thighs, and he started begging. "Please" and "more" and "fuck, yeah" fell out of him, but Max had stopped paying attention to his mouth because his brain was focused on every tender brush of cool skin against his. Rick's fingers whispered across his chest and thighs, but that strong tentacle up Max's ass was demanding. Unyielding.

Max was caught between those two storm fronts.

Max arched his back and came with a cry, his body one overstretched nerve as come shot out and splattered across his lower stomach. Rick trembled and twitched, his tentacles tightening until Max had trouble breathing. Max tried to speak, but couldn't catch his breath and he panted as the orgasm left him feeling about as energetic as a beached fish.

Rick pulled his tentacle out, leaving Max hollow. "You are damn good at this sex thing," Max finally managed to say.

Rick caressed Max's neck before settling his weight down against Max's side. Max fought his lethargy to pull Rick closer to him. Their bodies pressed together, Rick's cooler skin a balm against Max's heat. "I test Max body. I like Max body."

"I like Rick body," Max said. There was so much more he wanted to say. He wanted to reassure Rick that he cared more about him than he ever had any other creature in his life. He wanted to stand in front of a judge and promise "until death do us part." Ironically, he wanted a white picket fence and a little house, even though they lived on a spaceship with three kids who would not want to live on Earth.

But Max was too tired to sort all his feelings. He would settle for having Rick in his life forever. That was all he needed.

Chapter Fifteen

Kohei came into the room, moving fast enough that Max abandoned the computer model of Tribes armor he was designing. Carrington's lead warrior now understood the value of having weapons caches on board, and he needed to strike while the purse strings were open and the Tribes people were thinking about invasions and the need to stockpile a few supplies. "Max Father, a human wants to come into the ship." He blasted the words loudly enough that he sounded like James.

For a second, Max could only stare. "What?" he asked.

Kohei rotated a quarter turn. "Query to clarify."

Max stood. "Query. Did you say a human? Are you sure?"

Kohei blew raspberries. "I know species of father mine. Is human. Two boned leg tentacles with unbalanced walk. Small head very far off body. Two boned arm tentacles with only three major joints. Long, oddly placed finger tentacles. Human."

That was a creepy description of humanity, but accurate as well. "Where? The main door?" Max trotted past Kohei on his way to the elevator. "Query. What name did he give?"

"Asking of name intimate. I am no rude."

Max stopped in the elevator and forced himself to wait for Kohei to get all his tentacles inside when he wanted to hit the urgent button on the thing. "Wait. Do all species consider asking for a name rude?"

"Clarify. Query. Statement was query?"

"Yes, that was a question." Kohei did not have Xander's familiarity with the language, but then again, he was the child Max had ignored, so that was his fault. "Query. Do all species consider asking for a name rude?"

"Many species," Kohei said. "Hidden people do not, but they will often give different names depending which personality to display. Other peoples often do equate rudeness with asking of name where name does not correlate with close relationship. Official designation is enough."

That had so many cultural bombshells in it that Max couldn't deal with all of them. For now, he cared about the human at his door. The elevator opened, and Max hurried out with Kohei trailing after him. "Query. Did the human leave his official designation?"

"Official designation: human seeking entrance to ship of Hidden people."

Max sighed. Gene Roddenberry must have been kidnapped by logical aliens at some point because aliens were more like Spock than coincidence could explain.

He opened the main door and froze. He stared at her and she stared at him, and both of them had their mouths hanging open. Max found his voice first. "Dee?"

"Max! Oh my God, it's you!" Dee had never been a touchy-feely person, but she threw herself at Max and caught him in a huge hug. Kohei went all curly fries, and then his tentacles got stiff and he moved forward.

"Dee! It's so good to see you. I saw your plane shot out of the sky." The second he said that, Max knew what had happened. Like with him, the aliens had plucked her out of the plane so she didn't die the way Dan had when debris tore through his parachute. "Fuck. Were you on the same police ship that took me in?"

"I have no idea," she said, "I was unconscious for a time, and then I hid in the world's tiniest room." She backed up a step and glared at Kohei. She probably figured he was eavesdropping.

Rather than dribble and drabble out the weirdness, Max decided to get it all out on the table. "Dee, this is Kohei. He is one of three offspring I was a surrogate for."

She looked stunned. This is why he had avoided his home planet... that and he might be arrested for desertion because he had chosen family over returning to the Air Force. Eventually she said, "Max" in a low, horrified voice.

Max didn't want his children exposed to even more prejudice, but he didn't want to tell Dee to go fuck herself. It was a difficult position. "Kohei, why don't you go in and ask James to look at the work I've done on the Tribes armor."

"Max Father," Kohei said. His tentacles were a confused mass of curly fry and stiff outrage.

"We're going to go for a walk and talk," Max said. "Go back and check with your brother."

Kohei placed two tentacle tips against Max's leg. "It's fine," Max promised. "Go back inside." Kohei's tentacles pulled up a little tighter, but he did turn back toward the elevator, and Max headed out of the ship. Only then did it occur to him that he wasn't armed. The news of a human visitor had knocked the common sense out of him. Well, they didn't have to go far, and if Max knew his family—and he did—they would be watching as long as he was in sight of the cameras. But the cultural taboo against listening in public would come in handy because Dee was about to say some heinous shit. He could tell from her expression.

In the air, she was focused, aggressive, direct. And that tended to be her conversational style, too. When she looked up from her book, she was grotesquely honest. They called her Ditzy because she was the polar opposite of that term.

"Let's go lean awkwardly against the informational kiosk," he suggested. Names, mass transit, and chairs. Aliens didn't know what they were missing.

Dee chuckled. "Yeah, I've spent lots of time wandering the streets, and I haven't yet found a decent place to sit. Do you think they do that to prevent people from congregating?"

"Or tentacles don't get tired like boned tentacles do."

"Boned tentacles. Yeah. I've heard that one." She leaned against the kiosk Max had pointed out and stared at Rick's ship. Max cleared his throat and tried to compose his thoughts. He thought it was hard communicating with aliens, but humans left him equally tongue-tied.

"Hey, I get it," she said. "You do what you have to do. Isn't that what they taught us in those survival classes? I'm not judging."

Funny. Her promise not to judge made him feel pretty damn judged. "When I took the job, the translator said I would be a nanny."

She snorted.

"It was the only job that paid enough that I would have some hope of getting home."

Her face contorted. "Yeah." Her sigh was soul-deep. "I would have taken the job, too. Up until two days ago, I was working as a translator for pennies. Of course, that was before I was told the work was no longer necessary because someone had a much more complete human translation interface than the sad attempt I had made. Now I'll have to find another crap job. If someone told me that I could get home by acting as a surrogate for one of those parasites, I would have."

The word hit Max like a punch. "Whoa. Rick and the kids are not parasites."

Dee's expression turned slightly pitying. "They lay eggs in the bodies of other animals. I'm fairly sure that's the technical definition of parasite."

"They ask before laying eggs and pay quite well. Humans hire surrogates all the time. Are we parasites?"

"Um, we have the ability to have our own children. The Uglies literally can't give birth to their own children. And if one wanted to have a child and couldn't pay a surrogate, don't you think they would put their eggs in someone anyway? In fact, as I understand it on their home planet they raise animals specifically for the purpose of carrying their young."

Max crossed his arms over his chest. "As I understand it," he said, mirroring her words, "humans raise animals for the sole purpose of killing them, ripping their bodies apart, and then eating pieces."

She had the grace to look chagrined. "That does sound bad."

"I'm fairly sure that every sentient species is going to sound psychopathic if you describe them honestly enough." That did not say good things about the nature of sentient life, but Max was pretty sure he was right. Maybe it took a certain level of aggression to reach space. But of all the species Max had read about, the Hidden ones were the least psychotic of the bunch. Either that or Rick was hiding the really embarrassing informational tapes.

"Okay, okay. I am working on the required mental adjustments here," she promised. "They're sort of creepy. I mean, if you have one, it can have sex with itself and then drop hundreds of eggs in hundreds of different animals and the next thing you know, the planet is buried in Ug— Hidden ones."

"Have they done that?" Nothing in Rick's nature suggested that he would shove eggs into an animal and walk away. He had hovered over Max and even though he kept a certain distance from the children, he would shiver in pleasure when Max described how well they were doing in their studies. He was a proud papa octopus.

"Not that I've read about," she admitted. "But I haven't heard of anyone actually having spider eggs erupt from their bodies, and that is still an ongoing nightmare of mine. Sometimes the possibility is enough to give someone the creeps." She shivered dramatically.

"Rick is my common-law husband," Max said.

Her mouth fell open. Literally. He could've counted her teeth if he'd wanted to. He didn't.

"When he found out that I had misunderstood the job description, he offered to abort the children. He was a big ball of curled up tentacles and misery, but he would have done that if I wanted. He respected that I had a choice about whether or not to have babies in me."

She opened her mouth without speaking, closed it, and then cleared her throat. "So, he wasn't a sick fuck who knocked you up and forced you to carry his children, so you married him?"

And that was the Dee Max knew and generally tried to avoid. "No, that's when I looked at him as a person and not an employer. He's kind and a giant worry wart and a good father and weirdly obsessed with Darth Vader and Jar Jar Binks."

"What? How the hell does he know about *Star Wars*?"

A half-second too late, Max realized that he didn't want Dee to know how close he had been to Earth. Being stranded was one thing, but she would not approve of his plan to go AWOL... or rather to stay AWOL. "I like to tell them stories. By the way, I've told them the version where Jar Jar is a secret sith who uses the drunken monk martial arts to make everyone underestimate him. So if they start talking to you about Jar Jar, be prepared for weirdness."

Both her eyebrows were making a run for her hairline. "So this Hidden one," and boy couldn't Max hear the air quotes around that, "likes Darth Vader and sith infiltrators and you think he's a keeper?"

"He's equally obsessed with Galen Erso and Buffy Summers."

"Who?"

"Galen Erso. The Empire forced him to help design the death star, so he built it in a way to destroy it and then gave the plans to the rebellion, and Buffy Summers is the vampire slayer."

She studied him for several long minutes. "You watch too much TV."

"I did before I enlisted. Afterward, I didn't have enough time to truly indulge my addiction." He grinned at her, but she did not seem to appreciate his humor.

She rubbed a hand over her face. "Look, I get that this Hidden one has been kind and that you have an emotional connection to its kids. I get that." She took a breath.

Max jumped in before she could say anything more offensive than the shit she had already said. "Don't even assume this is some sort of fucking Stockholm syndrome. Rick hired me. He didn't threaten me, and when Hunter aliens invaded the ship, I protected my family because they are my family."

She leaned closer. "But did you have a choice? I know what it feels like to be alone. I get it. Aliens are not exactly touchy-feely sorts. I always thought of myself as an introvert, but I am crawling out of my own skin without someone to talk to, someone to touch or hear laugh." Her voice projected more desperation. "It's so fucking hard that my head aches with the pressure of being alone most of the time. However, the Uglies are not your only choice. The main docks have small living quarters that anyone can claim for the night. They're clean and secure. And food is free if you don't mind bland staples. Living with this alien is not your only choice. You can have a decent life here. I'll show you the ropes. And now that the translation computer works, maybe there will be more opportunities... other opportunities. You can't limit yourself to one plan. There will be other ways to get home." She caught his hand in hers and held on with a strength that startled Max.

He stared at her, horrified by the pain he could see reflected in her features, but repulsed by the suggestion that he should choose her over his family. He squeezed her hands back and wondered how long it had been since she touched anyone. Had anyone offered her any kindness? His heart warred with two obligations. He couldn't abandon her, but he couldn't expose his children to the sort of casual prejudice she was showing.

"I love them," Max said gently. "Come get to know them. Eventually we will have the money to fly back to Earth, and you can come with us."

She backed away a step. "You have to know how much those things creep me out."

Max loved Dee the way he loved all the guys in his unit. These were the people he'd trained with, fought with, drank with. He knew them better than he knew his biological family, and lots of spouses got jealous of how close the guys in the unit were. However, he would not choose her over his family. "You can't come into my house and insult the children I'm raising," he said firmly. "*My* children."

"You can't—"

Max didn't wait to find out what she thought he couldn't do. "I'm happy to introduce you to Rick if you can be polite, but I don't want to argue with you, and I have work I need to finish. I've convinced a trader that her ship has security vulnerabilities, so now I hope to make a little money by selling her equipment to fill in those gaps. Come back in three or four hours, and we can share some food and you can meet Rick." He backed away from her.

He read shock in her expression. As Max retreated, that transformed to dismay. Max turned and fled up the ramp to the ship before the guilt made him do something stupid... like invite her to move in with them so she didn't have to be alone.

He didn't have to trigger the door mechanism or wait for it because Kohei stood watching through a crack in the door. As Max approached, he moved back and the door slid open. Max ran home.

Chapter Sixteen

Max leaned against the equipment cart and watched Carrington's head of security lower the weapon. "What do you think?" he asked.

"It is an excellent improvement," she said.

Max had no idea if she was a she, but the Tribes aliens with their elaborate dress and triangular faces made him think female. He was a horrible person for making that assumption, but Max didn't have the energy to worry about his lack of woke-ness right now. He had a con to run, and so he let his brain make the assumption that Tribes aliens were very tall women with muscular, jointed necks.

Besides, if asking for a name was taboo, then asking about reproductive organs seemed whatever level was two steps beyond taboo. Scandalizing maybe. Infuriating was a possibility. And Max did not want to infuriate this Tribes alien he had nicknamed Xena. She had grasped the mechanics of the weapon and had proved a deadly shot. She would not have fallen for the same shit the Hunter aliens had, so either their prowess at hunting was overrated or Tribes aliens were skilled warriors as well as willing to take jobs as social workers. It was almost human of them.

"I'm glad you approve. I brought some armor for you to try on as well," Max said as she took another shot. She didn't even line it up. She lifted and fired in one motion. And she still hit the target. *Damn.*

Xena craned her neck around one hundred and eighty degrees, and Max suppressed an instinctive shudder. She said, "That word did not translate. Clarify armor."

"Armor is protective clothing that is used to counter the weapons of others." Now that English had been added to the business translation computer and an obscene amount of compensation had been added to Max's bank account, communication was easier, but not perfect. And more annoying, Rick did not have an expensive business computer license. So the one person Max yearned to freely communicate with, he couldn't.

He could if he and Rick were somewhere like Carrington's ship, but if they were on her ship, they couldn't do half of the things they wanted to. Maybe a quarter because Max did like to do a lot of things other than have sex. He would enjoy being able to discuss whether or not Buffy the Vampire Slayer should have made Xander come out of the closet without a lack of emotional context and translation matrix failure. The more he had that improved communication with other aliens, the more he ached to share it with Rick.

However, they had researched the price of a license, and even their much-improved budget couldn't handle that sort of expense. It would compromise their ability to buy supplies and update the computers. And since Rick made his living with those computers, the updates had to come first. And improved security and engines came second, and the translation computer was far enough down on their wish list that Max didn't think about it. Or he tried not to.

The door opened and a rush of humidity flooded the room. Xena turned around and put the weapon on Max's equipment cart before lowering her head in respect. That turned her neck into a broken S-shape, and Max looked away as a cold shiver shot up his spine.

"I see you are seeking to improve your financial position through my credits again," Carrington said. The gill slits on her neck quivered.

"I do provide the best weaponry out there. I assume you want the best."

"I am very concerned about claiming the best of everything."

Max had named her well when he'd called her Carrington. Her love for oversized hats and her desire to own nice things were the two constants he could count on from her. He found her much more relaxing to be around than Bundy. He understood Bundy and found him useful. Given that Bundy was making a ton of money acting as their representative, Bundy had started sucking up.

But there was something about Carrington that struck Max as human. Download her brain into Alexis Carrington's body, and she could've walked the streets of Denver, and no one would know the difference. It was nice to be around an alien that Max felt like he could predict.

For example, he had predicted Carrington would drop in on the sales call. Max hadn't asked for her, and theoretically, he was meeting with Xena to discuss arms and equipment. However, the second Rick had registered his program in Max's name, Max knew that Carrington was going to make an appearance. And he could even predict what she was going to do.

"I enjoy being compensated for my work. But then, I think that's a universal sentiment. I don't know of anyone who likes to be underpaid."

"I consent." Carrington bent her neck downward, and Max avoided the sight of that unnatural curve. Still reminded him of a bird's broken neck. "I acknowledge you registered a copyright on a new program this morning."

Bingo. That is exactly where Max had expected this conversation to go.

"I did," he said in a mild tone. "That has been my main project for months. I work on arms and more physical projects when I need to take a break."

"Even when you were carrying the Ugly offspring?" Carrington blinked at him.

"Even when I was pregnant with the Hidden offspring," he corrected her.

Her gills quivered.

"Anyway, I am letting Bundy handle the auction on that program. I don't know what the navigation program is worth."

Carrington moved closer. "I have the ability to administrate the sale," she said.

What a beautifully greedy bitch she was. Max loved it. Feeling almost as if he was back on Earth, he shook his head. "I have an agreement with Bundy. I won't go back on my word to him."

She stood straight, her neck lengthening. "Are you aware that only sentience that is capable of producing a protector can deeply understand honor? Other species only know words and rules and laws of honor." She looked at Xena. Xena tilted her head to the side and turned so she showed the underside of her chin.

Max packed the weapons away. He doubted he could get Xena to purchase any body armor, not with Carrington making her play for the bigger prize. "That's interesting. I imagine you have psychologists who spend their lives comparing the thought processes of different species. That would be an interesting career." Max would've rather scooped out his own brain, but someone would find it fascinating. "I trust that you have honor because I believe you will not manufacture weapons without purchasing the rights even though Xena understands every alteration I have made."

"I do," Xena agreed. "I would not have thought of such changes, but seeing them, I understand the theory and function. I will pay you because you have brought value to these weapons and I will not dishonor value."

"I appreciate that." And Max did. It was good to know that Carrington's crew didn't plan to cheat him.

Carrington slid another inch closer, and Max was uncomfortable with her proximity. He suspected she was trying to buddy up to him to get the profits from the navigation program. "You have brought value to navigation. That value is not as obvious to understand."

"I'm not going to cut Bundy out of the deal." Max wanted the buyers hungry and competitive before bidding started. That was why he had come out to show Xena his newest weapon design. People wanted what was right in front of them, and Max needed to be in front of the prospective buyers to make them want the program more. He was going to go visit Tweedle Dee and Tweedle Dum later. The two Pajekhs had purchased his first weapon and had asked him to do a security check on their ship. Their language was closer to human and less likely to give Max a headache, but the *Spaceballs* aliens left him trying to avoid giggling. But they had credits, and Max planned to let them try to lure him into selling them a copy under the table. He wouldn't because that would undermine the final auction price, but he would let them make their play so they could taste that program and want it even more.

Luckily greed was universal. Even Bundy had to admit that Max was good at marketing his work.

"You have honor. But you do not have obligation of honor to Bundy," Carrington said. "He is buyer and seller. He has no honor to you."

"Oh, I am sure you're right about that," Max said. Bundy would've stabbed him in the back for a credit. Or at least have done the financial equivalent. "But he took a chance on my work when everyone else thought I was a moron."

"You are a warrior. Warriors and protectors are not morons," Xena bellowed.

"Thank you." Max appreciated the support. "But a lot of people made assumptions." Max didn't add that the people on the law-enforcement ship had no business doing any sort of assessment of new species because they were morons.

"Both humans in custody appeared to lack cognitive skills," Carrington said. "That is evidence in support of claim. Not assumption."

Max flinched at the mention of Dee. She had not come back that night or in the week since she had visited. He felt like an ass for not running after her, for not doing something to make her see that his family would welcome her and she didn't have to be alone. He couldn't imagine what her life had been like at the docks. She said nightly lodging and food were free, but man or woman couldn't live by reconstituted vitamin cubes alone. Hell, she didn't even have a volleyball she could paint a face on. He remembered sitting in the maintenance shaft and crying because he felt so damn lonely, and he hadn't been alone.

She had.

"We were injured and had too many new ideas introduced at once. I hear the Chosen did not handle it well when they learned of other sentient life in the universe."

Xena made a bugling noise.

Carrington tilted her head. "You speak factually."

"Thank you. I like to be factual." Max locked the equipment cart before picking up the remote. It was time for him to go home.

"Humans are factual." Carrington repeated herself. Max turned on the cart and started it toward the exit. Damn, this ship was humid. Max would have to change clothes when he got home because he had just about sweated through this one. He could have entered a wet T-shirt competition with it.

Carrington walked beside him. She was persistent. "Being factual, you should understand well that I would handle your sales more effectively."

"I am happy with the effectiveness of Bundy." Max smiled at her. He wondered if she took that as a friendly or threatening gesture. He didn't care, but he did increase the speed of the equipment cart.

"There are facts which make me an improved administrator of your sales. There are facts that would endanger your ability to make sales," she said as she followed him.

Max didn't stop the cart, but he stopped to study her for a second before turning his attention back to it before he drove it into a wall. "That sounds slightly mobbish."

"Clarify the term mobbish," she said.

"Mob. Dishonorable individuals who work together to break the law or earn compensation by making others feel threatened or threatening them." Huh. Max was getting good at being a dictionary.

Carrington's neck gills slapped shut. "I am not lacking honor."

"I never said you were," Max said before he could drive his best customer away. "Your statement sounded like a threat, so the statement sounded mobbish, not you."

Carrington followed as Max approached the main exit. Fresh air from outside leaked through the thick ship air like water through a sieve, assuming that water seeped through that sieve in such small quantities that a person was desperate for more. The humidity was killing Max. "From a certain perspective, perhaps," Carrington admitted. "I dislike how humans see perspective."

Max laughed. "We are annoying," he agreed. He increased the cart's speed now that he saw the open door.

"I would ensure you compensation beyond the ensuring of honorless Bundy," Carrington tried again. She was the most persistent alien ever. Well, other than Rick, but that didn't count because Max liked Rick.

"Max!" a voice called out in English. For a half second, Max feared Xander had followed him, but Xander's voice was lower and more sing-song than clipped like this one. Dee raced toward him. "Run!" she screamed.

Max's feet engaged before he could consider motives or possibilities. His squad member told him he had to run, so he dropped the cart's remote and sprinted toward the exit. A Tribes alien came out of a side door, and Max went into a controlled slide, his feet forward, the sides of them digging up the slime that covered the ship's floor. He hit the Tribe's alien in the ankle, and with a bugle, the creature went down.

It scrambled to catch Max, but all it caught was the edge of a shirt that ripped when Max jerked free. He dashed for the open air, but the second he broke free, he spotted the line waiting for him. People of Red, their violet stripes and lips—their operatic cries as they spotted Max—their law-enforcer uniforms. Oh fuck. Something had gone wrong.

A body crashed into him from behind, and then human hands clutched his arm. "Oh fuck," Dee whispered, an echo of his own thoughts. Yep, that about summed it up. An alien raised a stunning weapon, and Max raised his hands in surrender.

Chapter Seventeen

Max followed the lead law-enforcement alien, but most of his attention was on Dee who walked beside him. He had no idea what she had done, but she had done something. He knew it. He kept glaring at her, but she was immune because she didn't even bother looking chagrined.

Carrington's ship was closer to the city, and that was where they were headed. It meant that every step took him farther from his family. Max wondered how long Rick would wait for him to return before he figured out that something was wrong. Selfishly, Max wished Rick were here to curl a tentacle around his arm and tell him that he knew how to fix this.

Not that Rick would say that. Rick would bugle complaints about Max never listening to his warnings. He would probably then add a few insults about Max not running fast enough. Even if Rick berated him for following this stupid plan, Max would want him here. And to be honest, Rick had a right to say "I told you so" about a thousand times.

They passed the three- and four-story buildings that housed traders and craftsmen and headed deeper into the city, always surrounded in front and back by the purple People of the Red. At one point, they passed an alley, and Max considered making a run for it, but when they got to the entrance, a police officer stood in the opening, his oversized lips moving with *puck-puck-puck* sounds.

At five feet tall, it wasn't impressive, but its weapon was. Bundy had tried to convince Max that weapons weren't valuable commodities. He was either an optimist or an idiot. And the whole time, aliens stepped aside to watch as Max and Dee were escorted by the armed guards. As they passed, the chatter would quiet, and huge alien eyes would watch them pass.

They passed under an archway, and the boardwalk broadened and the buildings grew taller. Max had never been to this part of the city. Fuck. Max glared at Dee, but this time she narrowed her eyes and glared back at him. "Don't give me shit because I warned you too late for you to get out," she snapped at him. She lifted her chin and probably hoped to project strength, but that was not the impression Max got.

A forward guard turned to consider them, and hysterical giggles floated through Max's gut. Rick would have told the guard that it lacked eyes in appropriately asymmetrical rear-facing places.

No matter what had happened, the police were treating both of them the same. By trying to help Max, Dee had landed in the soup with him. Max waited until the guard turned back to the front before he leaned closer to Dee and whispered, "What did you tell people about me?" If he could figure out what he was being charged with, maybe he could minimize the damage.

She narrowed her eyes more. "I didn't tell them anything. I overheard them talking about you."

"And you happened to be on Carrington's ship?" That was too much coincidence.

Dee's anger vanished and she looked confused. "Carrington?" They both fell silent when an eight-foot-tall alien with a crown of tentacles took a step forward. A People of Red alien screeched, and the translator gave a sharp "Back!" The aggressive alien retreated, but Dee couldn't stop staring at it.

Max was more concerned about the Hunters in the curious crowd. None of them came near, but Max's palms itched with the ghost of a maintenance hook slick with viscera.

Max pulled his thoughts away from that morbid subject. "Carrington. The alien who owns that ship. Big hat, money hungry... you know, Alexis Carrington."

"You give them names?" Shock colored Dee's voice. "I mean, I knew you gave names to the ones you called family, but you name all of them?" She studied him as if Max were ten cards short of a full deck.

Max took offense at her tone. "What do you do?"

"Random alien one, random alien two, random alien three." She shrugged. "And then there's the big alien with the weird neck who hired me to translate technical specifications into Earth math. And since your translation program made my last job obsolete, getting this job seemed like a godsend."

Max's heart sank. "Technical translator?"

Dee glanced at the front guard, but they were marching toward the city center. They might have been short, but they were all legs under a round elf-body, so they could keep up a good pace. And they didn't seem to care that their two prisoners were comparing stories. They sucked as police officers.

Dee edged closer and lowered her voice. "They showed me a lot of technical theories and practical applications and asked me to explain the math in human terms. Some of it made absolutely no sense at all, some of it violated every theory of physics that I know, and some of it made sense if I squinted and tilted my head to the right three degrees."

Oh fuck. Max had underestimated Carrington. At least he assumed Carrington had arranged all this. If that was his hypothesis, he needed to test it. "Did they have you translate specifications for a weapon?"

"Yeah. That one I could almost understand," Dee said. "It focused a beam of energy. You totally would have been into it because it had science fiction written all over it."

There was a compliment in there somewhere, but Max was too freaked-out to care. "What else were you translating?" Max's guts were turning to stone. "Were there any programs related to navigation?"

"Shields, navigational programs, energy usage in engines, energy dispersal patterns on what might be some sort of tac vest, all sorts of things." She shrugged as if she hadn't confirmed Max's worst fears.

"Like I said, most of it didn't make any sense, and if the autopilot they showed me is accurate, I have no idea why their ships don't slam straight into the nearest port because I do not understand how they are compensating for the gravitational mass of nearby objects. But then, we aren't all dead, so their ships have to be compensating somehow." She laughed, but the sound had a hard edge.

Max had stopped listening somewhere around the time she'd said navigational program. That bitch. Max had named her entirely too accurately. She had hired someone to prove that Max was not the author of all of the programs he was offering. It was the only thing that made any sense. But the problem was, that didn't make a lot of sense. Why the hell did she care whether or not he wrote the program? She was running an angle, but he couldn't figure out how bringing in law enforcers helped advance her position.

And he couldn't figure out how any of this explained Dee's actions. "Translating technical specifications doesn't seem like a good reason to yell at me to run," Max said. "Why did you think I was in danger?"

"I wouldn't say danger," Dee said.

Max gave her an incredulous look. "You came bolting out of a side corridor door and screamed at me to run. That sounds like danger, and as someone who was stationed very briefly in a war zone, I know what danger sounds like."

"No one was shooting or threatening to shoot." Dee grimaced. "I might have overreacted, but I had a gut feeling."

Given that they were under guard and walking toward the city center like the universe's slowest, saddest parade, her gut was in good working order.

"An alien I was working with showed me a new program, and it had weird-ass mathematical symbols. When I asked the computer to clarify them, I got back essentially gobbledygook. I told them the math didn't exist on Earth."

Max already knew that much. Even when Rick tried to explain in simple terms, all Max ever got was belches and whale song and aspersions about human intelligence in general, which Rick would then immediately follow up by repeatedly saying that Max was a not-moron, even if his species couldn't find space with a dozen tentacles. "That doesn't explain why you believed I was in danger."

"One of the aliens turned to another, and said, 'I knew it. Go tell him before the human leaves the ship.'"

Well, that ended any lingering hope that this was a big misunderstanding fueled by alien confusion over why Max had tried running. Now he needed to figure out how to minimize the legal liability.

He hoped aliens had some version of Miranda rights. After all, they did have some sense of justice as evidenced by the fact that they had given him a social worker of sorts. But that sense of justice was limited. Dee had been on the same ship with him, and they had never seen each other. That had been a dick move on the crew's part. Serious dick move, and Dee had suffered for that way more than Max. It wasn't lost on him that she wasn't even trying to name aliens or have relationships with individuals.

And then there was the whole shady habit of discriminating against Hidden ones. The universe had no problem screwing people over on a monumental scale. And since Max allied himself with Hidden ones, he suspected some of the perceived cooties were going to land on him. That was the way it worked in racist societies. Straight people could love the *Queer Eye* guys and tell people to sashay away without any repercussions, but gay guys were effeminate or flaming or shoving their sexuality in other people's faces if they did the same damn things. Sentient life sucked. The longer Max lived, the more he joined team Thanos.

"Don't say anything to anyone until we figure out what the legal recourse is," Max whispered as he spotted uniformed aliens standing outside a building that had impractical spires and fantastical angles.

Her eyebrows went up. "Legal recourse?" She leaned closer. "What the hell are you involved with?"

"Nothing unethical." He couldn't claim nothing illegal since he didn't know the wider universe's views on running cons. If they were on Earth, nothing he had done would be illegal. Of course, given that Nathan Ford would have approved of these schemes, there was an implication that he was skirting the edges of the law a bit. He was about to find out how this part of the universe viewed scofflaws.

"Great," Dee muttered sarcastically.

The guards ushered them up a set of shallow steps toward a metallic blue building. Max couldn't have agreed with her more.

Chapter Eighteen

Max paced the length of the narrow room where he'd been placed. Compared to a spaceship, it was downright palatial; however, he still didn't have room to do more than pace twelve steps in one direction before he had to turn and pace the same twelve steps back.

A narrow slot window gave him a view of most of the sprawling city, but they were up high enough that Max couldn't see any detail. Even the ships were tiny models fit only for grasshoppers and ants, that was how far up he was. The misty clouds were a beauty filter over the entire sprawling metropolis.

Cables ran from one tower to another, and small cars zipped along. Max suspected they were as much to support the great heights of the inner towers as to provide transportation for people who didn't feel like going down a mile to the ground to walk a few hundred feet and then go another mile up into the air. He might be exaggerating with a mile, but it felt like it.

On the good side, he had finally seen what he thought was alien mass transit. There were concentric rings that vanished out of the narrow line of sight the window offered. At each of those rings, the nature of the city changed. Max's tower prison faced the direction of the spaceport, which was outside those rings.

In fact, the outermost ring was broken, leaving a gap for the spaceport and crowded marketplace of traders. Maybe the rest of the city didn't want to make it too easy for the trash that came in with the ships to get to their core community.

And maybe Max was putting human motives onto aliens, something which never ended well. For example, he had assumed that

Carrington would want access to the various programs Max could sell her. So he had assumed it would be counterproductive for her to report to the authorities that his programs were beyond the scope of human capability. Sure, he thought blackmail was possible, but not this counterproductive involvement of the authorities when the program hadn't sold yet. Or maybe Carrington and Bundy were in it together and they were going to steal the program.

Max sat on the edge of the world's narrowest bunk and dropped his head into his hands. He was so screwed. The only way into the cell was an elevator, there were no door controls or access panels, and even if his captors had left the wiring out for him to poke around in, he didn't know how to hot wire an alien door. The window was equally worthless as an escape route.

It meant he was stuck. All he could do was figure out a plan to minimize the danger to the rest of his family. And he would do that as soon as he knew what the danger was. He now knew why Hannibal Smith and Nate Ford avoided personal relationships. Putting others in danger was so much harder than walking into it himself. Well that and the writers had a bad habit of killing all the women who got too close to a lead in a male-dominated series, but Max was fairly sure that had more to do with the general suckiness of American culture than the inherent danger of running a con and being in love.

The door set into the long wall of his cell beeped, and Max turned toward it. Either aliens weren't worried about elevator breakdowns, or they didn't give a shit if prisoners were stranded during a fire. Then again, given how high up they were, having access to a stairway wouldn't be much of an improvement.

The door opened and Max only realized he had dropped into a fighting stance when he let his hands fall to his sides. Kohei walked through the door. Kohei. Yep, those were Kohei's giant freckles and his streaks of mint-green.

"What are you doing here?"

"I come to see you, Max Father," Kohei said. Oh thank god, the fancy translator was turned on.

"Is the family safe?"

"Stupid James wants to shoot stupid people."

"Well don't let him!" Fuck. Max was going to give that idiot a tongue-lashing to be the end of all parental tongue-lashings if he even tried taking on an entire fucking planet of enemies.

"Rick Father locked controls and put all weapons away. Xander called him stupid."

"Maybe don't call him 'stupid' to his face," Max suggested. He knew when his dad called his ideas dumb, he tended to double down on whatever dumb-ass plan he was working on.

Kohei came the rest of the way into the room and the door closed. With one of the kids in the middle, Max couldn't even rush the door. Kohei continued. "I promised to listen if stupid people don't stop seeking to advance their own stupidity."

Max snorted. The problem was that the aliens weren't actually stupid. They hadn't fallen for Max's con. "What are they charging me with?" Once Max knew he could start to figure out how to jack himself out of this hole, or he could resign himself to it.

"Max Father, they do not accuse you of any crime."

"Really? This feels a lot like a prison cell." Max gestured to the room as a whole.

"I have seen Earth prison cells. This does not appear equivalent." Kohei slid toward the window. "This has much better view."

Max's children were annoyingly logical. "Yes, but this also has a locked door."

"Most doors are locked against people walking where walking is unwise."

Max frowned. Maybe he wasn't as screwed as he'd thought. But... "They brought me here using guards with guns."

Kohei's tentacles curled up a bit, and they should. Max did not appreciate being threatened like that. "Did you kill guards?" Kohei asked.

Max raised his eyebrows. "That's the sort of question your Rick Father might ask, and your Rick Father is paranoid about my past as a warrior." Kohei's tentacles relaxed, and Max shook his head. "Just because I know how to fight doesn't mean I fight everyone. Besides, I was outnumbered."

"You were outnumbered by Hunters, and you killed," Kohei said.

Max had to admit that had there not been so many guards he might have considered trying to fight his way through. He probably would've gotten his ass kicked, but he would've tried. "I had the advantage being on my home turf, and they didn't give me a choice. I tried cooperating, and they were going to kill us anyway."

Kohei's tentacles twitched. Hard. "I believe authorities have concern over reports that humans are warriors, so they send many escorts in case humans make troubles."

At least they respected his ability to defend himself. That was more respect than most Marines gave him. "Why were they escorting us? You keep saying I'm not under arrest, but this feels like an arrest. And where is Dee? They separated us."

"I am ignorant of location of Dee, but I understand the reason for the escorting. The authorities have accused Rick Father of manipulating a moron species in order to avoid sanction penalty on his navigation program. They also accuse Rick Father of being the source of weapon modification and armor that Max Father sold to others."

"Oh fuck."

Kohei's tentacles snapped up into coils. "Translator translated oddly," he said with a bugle.

It took Max a half second to realize that the computer must have translated the word fuck literally. That was a glitch he had fixed in the translator on the ship, but for all its improvements, the trading translator needed fine-tuning. "I meant that only as a general expression of dismay."

Kohei's tentacles uncurled. "Dismay is appropriate, Max Father. Rick Father is distraught."

"Fuck." Max sank onto the narrow cot. "What do the authorities want to do?" If they touched one finger on Rick's smallest tentacle, Max was going to demonstrate the term "homicidal rage."

"They wish to take Rick Father's everything." Kohei moved closer and brushed a tentacle across Max's arm. Max caught the tentacle and used it to pull Kohei close enough to hug. Kohei's tentacles wound around Max's neck and then Kohei was pulling hard enough that Max almost got dragged to the floor. He braced himself as Kohei hauled his bulk up into Max's lap and then curled his walking tentacle around Max's waist. Xander was the only one who had ever wanted to sit in Max's lap before, but if Max's mother had been there, he would have had the same urge.

He wanted to curl up in someone's lap while they figured this out. However, he was the parent, and now he had to pretend to have the situation under control when it was one giant FUBAR. He held Kohei and rocked the way he had when Xander had been small... all of three or four month ago. They grew up so fast.

"I need information. We have to save the family, and that means I need you to tell me everything. Why do they think they have a right to take the ship? What will the authorities do? What will Rick do? Is there any way to get a lawyer?"

Kohei kept his leg tentacle tight around Max's waist. "They believe Rick Father will flee. They hope to take the ship before he can."

"They think he will flee?" When Kohei didn't respond, Max realized that he thought Max was simply repeating information. "Query, why do they think Rick Father will flee?"

"Every instinct tells Rick Father and Xander and James and Kohei to flee. Hide. Preserve as many tentacles as possible from predators. But

Max Father is here, and that is like having walking tentacle caught by big predator and James is lashing tentacles and Rick Father is doing math and I am here and Xander is making words that are not words."

Max leaned back so he could see at least a couple of Kohei's eyes. "I need to speak with an authority. I want the right to argue my case that Rick Father did nothing wrong. Humans believe in the right to defend ourselves with words."

"I will call for..." And once again, Max was treated to untranslated whale-song. He had to assume from the context that Kohei knew what Max was asking for.

"Then, I need you to give Rick Father a message."

Kohei loosened his hold enough that he could rotate so a larger eye was centered on Max.

"If the authorities don't listen, if they keep trying to blame Rick and take his ship away, I want you to tell him to run. Hide. Do not wait for me or give the authorities anything to save me. If I know that any of you are suffering because of me, I will be far more hurt than anything the authorities can do to me."

"But Max Father—"

"Nope. If I can get free, I will come to the Hidden Planet, but you tell Rick Father he has to take care of himself and you kids. That is priority number one. I can take care of myself."

"Max Father!" Kohei bugled and all his tentacles tightened until they were almost choking Max. Max held on, wishing he could hug all his kids, desperately wishing he could hold Rick. However, his feelings didn't matter as much as protecting his family.

"You tell Rick Father that. Promise me you will give him that message exactly."

"I no wish to give such promise." Any tentacle not wrapped around Max was curled into a tight ball. Max could imagine primitive Hidden ones on their home world, hiding in some crevasse when a predator came too near.

"Promise me," Max demanded. "I will hurt more if I see you hurt. You can only protect me by protecting yourself."

After a long silence, Kohei said, "I hate promise, but I give it."

"I hate it, too, kiddo," Max said, and he hugged Kohei as tightly as he dared. "Me too, but we do what's right for the family."

Sometimes doing right sucked. Max wished the universe would stop trying to teach him that same lesson.

Chapter Nineteen

Max didn't know what he expected from an alien version of a competency hearing, but this wasn't it. The short wall opposite his narrow window was one huge screen, so it looked as if Max was in a cubby on the side of a large room. A few people glanced his way, so Max assumed the camera was projecting his image as well. He gave them credit for security. This setup gave Max zero opportunities to break out.

Aliens wandered in and out of circular benches that were interrupted by four aisles. Max's camera was lined up with one of those breaks, and he saw straight across to the opposite end of the room where an actual alcove sat empty.

The whole room was fifty feet by fifty feet, and there were far too many aliens in it for Max's comfort. He understood why some of the aliens were there. He spotted Carrington in an even more ridiculous hat than before, and Xena at her side. Bundy was on the far side of the room and he kept glancing toward Max before ignoring him. No doubt his bad mood had returned double. There were three pith-helmet Pajekh and many of the tall, nostrilly Chosen. The former were clustered in a group and the latter walked the room in a way that made Max think of guards or politicians.

A goose poop-green Smarties alien sat on the bench closest to Max's camera. Max wondered if that was the same one that had come to Bundy's meet-and-greet. And then there were a scattering of aliens Max didn't know. A green jellyfish with an enormous trunk and a set of tentacles growing out of the center of its head shifted to the right, and Max spotted two Hunter aliens, their orange pyramid bodies standing out in a room that had more greens and blues and purples.

Max's stomach heaved at the sight of them, and his hands itched with the memory of warm guts sliding over his skin. He shivered. And here he thought the day couldn't get worse. Whatever Max had done wrong in a previous life, it must have been bad. Really bad.

The aliens fell silent and turned toward Max's left. Instinct had Max moving closer to the wall to try to see around the corner, but of course that was an idiotic thing to do because he couldn't see around corners on a television screen. No wonder the aliens kept calling him an idiot.

Max's moment of levity as he silently made fun of himself vanished when Rick slid into the room. His tentacles were curled so tight that he was having trouble even walking, and Kohei walked next to him.

"What the fuck are you doing here? Oh hell no."

Rick and Kohei kept moving toward the center.

"Kohei, you promised you would give him my message. Rick! Rick!" Max screamed, but Rick didn't even rotate an eye in his direction. Someone had Max on mute.

"You turn the sound on right now so I can tell Rick exactly what I think of him coming here. I have a right to tell that moron to get back to his god damn ship. Do you hear me? I demand the right to talk to him. I must have some rights, and I fucking well demand them." Max screamed. Unsurprising, nothing happened.

A Chosen alien followed, and when Rick and Kohei sat on an inner bench, the Chosen one moved to the center and hauled his bulk up onto the table. Aliens sat on the closest bench and the table in the center turned ever so slowly. It gave Max a nice profile of that huge upper lip. So this was the judge.

It would have been awesome if someone had explained the proceedings to him, but the universe didn't have lawyers. The judge started wailing, and the volume on the microphone made Max flinch away from the screech. Luckily he only got a half second of that before the translated voice replaced it.

"The Tribes Carrington charges the Ugly Rick of manipulation of a moron species to circumnavigate the sanctions against Ugly planet." The judge gave that one sentence summary, then Carrington stood.

"The Human Porter cannot work any math the Human Max claims to have created and hopes to sell," she said. It took Max a half second to connect Human Porter to Dee, even when he knew that Dee's attempts to do technical translating had led to this mess. "The Human Max lives with the Ugly Rick. The Ugly planet is under sanctions."

She sat. The whole time, the table holding the judge rotated.

Bundy stood. "Human Max and Ugly Rick came together once with the weapon. Human Max had knowledge of weapon. Human Max came alone after that. The navigation program was registered to the Human Max." He sat.

If this was a trial, either humans or aliens had a truly fucked-up idea of what it meant to argue a position. They were focusing on facts, but facts meant nothing. They could mean anything. If a recruit had an AFOQT score of fifty, that could be good because it met the minimum standard for being selected for pilot training. It could be bad if only twenty slots were open and twenty other candidates had higher scores. It could be humiliating if the person had scored fifty-seven on a practice or exciting if it was the highest score a person had ever gotten. The test score was just a number. The context of that number was more important than the bare fact.

No one was trying to explain these facts.

The Smarties alien stood. "Human Max has separate account from Ugly Rick." It hunkered back down more than sitting.

Max saw the pattern. When the last person sat, someone in the judge's line of sight would stand and testify. So how long would she keep rotating, and would Max have a chance to speak? The speakers signaled that they wanted the floor by standing. Okay. Max could play this game.

He sat on the end of his narrow bench/bunk and prayed the judge allowed him to speak before Rick. Max adored Rick—loved him beyond all reason. However, Rick had the self-preservation instincts of a stoned lemming. No, a tweaking lemming. At least a stoned one would have the good sense to lie on the couch and do nothing. This idiot had left the safety of the ship to sit in a room full of aliens who were calling him ugly to his face.

Before getting kidnapped, Max had thought of himself as being pretty non-confrontational, or as non-confrontational as a fighter pilot could get. But now... he had fantasies about cutting off tentacles and oversized lips.

A Pajekh was speaking. "Human Max used credits from his account to install new sensors on the ship of Ugly Rick."

"Hey, that's our ship, thank you very much," Max muttered. The judge was turned in his direction, and Max stood.

"Can anyone hear me?"

Everyone turned toward him, so that was a yes. Max's face heated, and he didn't know why. It was a reasonable question. Max couldn't claim the navigation program was his, but maybe he could mitigate the damage. "I created the weapon because Hunters invaded my ship and I didn't like having to defend the ship and my family with a maintenance hook. I wanted a defense that would have less likelihood of me ending up dead. Can I ask a question of someone who is in the room?"

The judge's table stopped, and he had to shift around so he faced Max. Max got the feeling that this was not how it was supposed to work in this part of the universe. Tough shit. "On my planet, a trial like this often includes people asking each other questions. Can I do that?"

"Who would you ask a question of?" the judge asked.

"Tribes Xena."

"What question would you ask?" The judge seemed to push his lips out even farther, which elongated all the nostrils along the side of his nose and made him look sillier.

"I want her to describe her impressions of me when we worked together."

"That is not a question."

Damn logical aliens. "Did I seem to know what I was doing with weapons? Better?" Max stomped down on his temper before he said something that would earn him a contempt charge in a human court.

The judge's table began to rotate slowly again, and Max took his seat. Every court show he'd ever watched said that a lawyer should never ask a question he didn't know the answer to, but these assholes would never believe a word out of his mouth. They had already dismissed him as an idiot. He needed a character witness, one that the rest of the universe thought was pretty. When the judge swiveled toward Xena, she stood.

For a time, she was silent, and bile pressed at the base of Max's stomach. He couldn't defend Rick from a prison cell. What would happen to him if the authorities took their ship? Rick and the kids would be stranded here, surrounded by people who hated them. If Xena didn't tell the truth, Max didn't know how to convince these guys that he was competent to take the blame for his own actions.

"Human Max adequately explained the function of two different modifications to energy weapons, both of which will increase lethality. He also adequately explained the function of defensive garments he offered to sell and he identified weaknesses in the security of our ship and helped to design remediation plans." She sat so quickly that her hat flopped even though it was much smaller than Carrington's. Hopefully her testimony didn't create a problem with her boss, but Max couldn't care about that right now. Before the judge could swing back around to face him, Kohei stood.

Max held his breath. Better Kohei than Rick, but this was still the stuff of nightmares.

"I saw Human Max Father testing many weapons. He worked often with Ugly Xander Sibling. He brought human theories of weapon design to designs in the archives of the ship of Ugly Rick Father." He sat.

As much as Max knew that Kohei was playing it smart, Max hated hearing Kohei refer to family like that. They weren't ugly. Not even a little. They were graceful and beautiful and annoying, but never ugly. Max clenched his teeth and wished the judge were facing him. Instead the table stopped. No one stood. No one spoke. But the judge faced the far side of the room and the table did not budge.

Was the judge ready to make a decision? This felt arbitrary. Max hadn't gotten to say half the things he wanted to. But Rick and Kohei stayed seated. Max had to follow their lead because he had no idea what was going on.

He was going to research every fucking judicial process on every fucking planet when this was over. He hoped he wouldn't be locked in a cell while he did it, but according to television, researching legal cases was standard fare for the unjustly condemned. And television never lied.

Aliens shifted on their benches, some scooting sideways to get out of the judge's view. Ah. He was looking at the Hunters.

The larger one stood. "One ship of law-breakers reported that humans are irrational and dangerous when offspring are in danger." It sat. The judge remained motionless. Alien spectators inched away. The Hunters sat. It was the world's strangest standoff with silence being the major weapon. Max didn't understand why the judge assumed these Hunters would know about a pirate ship of Hunters, but then again, the universe focused on certain assumptions, like people didn't go to war against their own species. So maybe other species stuck together more than humans.

If so, the universe was in for a shock when humanity got this far, and they would. Max knew his people. As soon as they got their heads around the idea of aliens, they were going to build clunky, cramped spaceships so they could come up here and yell at them.

The Hunter stood, slower this time. "The human killed several Hunters and threatened death to Hunter Leader. He released Hunter Leader so Hunter Leader would take message back to all Hunters to avoid the ship with Ugly Offspring."

"Damn right," Max muttered even though no one could hear him. Several aliens did glance at him. The Hunter sat and the judge's platform started to rotate again.

An enormous alien stood. "Human Max hit my tentacle," he said before sitting. Damn. That was the guy who had tried to push past them on the boardwalk. Max had stepped on one of his tentacles. Okay, maybe it had been a stomp, but still. It seemed strange to come to court to tattle about something like that. Aliens were odd.

One of Bundy's customers stood and testified about Max's accuracy with weapons. Every time someone fell silent, the judge was facing away from Max, and he suspected that was intentional. People didn't want to hear what he had to say, but Max had a right to speak his mind. Or he didn't because this was an alien legal system and they had never heard of Miranda or the Constitution, but damn it, Max wanted to speak his mind.

He leaned forward, ready to leap from his seat, given the opportunity, but it never came. Instead alien after alien testified about Max's threats to cut off limbs and his habit of stepping on tentacles and his proficiency with weapons. This was going sideways. Rick had a right to two lifetimes of I-told-you-so.

Squirming in his seat, Max watched another alien sit, and then Kohei shot up even though he wasn't directly in front of the judge. However, no one said anything. Kohei waited until the judge had rotated the last degree or two before he told the story of Xander's birth and how Rick and Max had to keep him moving. He described such weird details, like how Max would stand in the water until the oils had washed away from his skin and the water soaked into his cells so his skin wrinkled. Personally, Max considered wrinkled skin pretty damn normal. He liked baths.

However, more and more, aliens turned to study Max. He was starting to feel like a bug pinned on a board.

Kohei rotated his largest eye toward Max and waited until the judge was turned in Max's direction before he sat.

Blessing Kohei's insight and strategy, Max leapt up. If he was going to be condemned as a psychopath instead of a moron, he had a few things to say to these aliens. And they were damn well going to listen. Hopefully.

Chapter Twenty

Max took a deep breath. If this was his only chance to speak, he needed to make it count, so he had to suppress the urge to run in a circle and scream in frustration. That wouldn't exactly disprove the theory that he was a moron.

"I came up with the concept for that weapon, and I had every right to sell it." Max remained as calm as possible. These people liked facts, so that was what he had to focus on. And he would apologize to James later for not giving him co-credit. "Dee would be able to do that math, only she has been isolated and afraid for so long that she probably can't think straight. And that would be the fault of the so-called smart individuals on that police ship. We were both on that ship, but instead of letting us see each other, the assholes on that ship kept up separated and confused."

Max took another calming breath. He was not doing well at remaining factual. It didn't help that he recognized the stress in Dee's eyes. In SERE training they said that nothing was more damaging than being alone. A person could handle broken bones better than systematic isolation. But these aliens wouldn't understand profanity, and if the translator was being too literal, Max's point would get lost under the verbal garbage.

"My people dislike most bodily fluids, and we have a special hatred for excrement. So when we find an individual as dislikable as excrement, we call them an asshole. The association of the body part with that particular bodily discharge makes our feelings known." Max had grown disturbingly good at that sort of explanation. Being a father had contributed to his new skills as much as the alien kidnapping. The kids did ask the strangest questions.

Back to his argument. "The people on the ship were assholes because they isolated us and didn't give us a chance to mentally recover from the shock." Max considered the closest Chosen alien. "Like some other species, many on my planet believed we were alone in the universe, that we were chosen by a deity to be unique. Others believed there was life in the universe, but could not prove it because our part of the galaxy was so quiet. So seeing alien ships was a shock." That was an understatement. "And those assholes saw shock and took it as proof that humans are morons. That sort of assumption makes the rest of you look like morons."

Max debated sitting. He had made his argument. However, he hadn't addressed the one part of his con that had outed him—that navigation program. Maybe he could convince these aliens that they had judged humans too quickly, but they'd had plenty of time to decide they didn't like the Hidden ones. So this part wouldn't end well. That ingrained hatred was going to make these guys assume that anyone who loved a Hidden one had to be a moron.

Looking at Rick sitting near the judge, his tentacles all curled, Max couldn't deny him. Not even by avoiding any mention of him.

"And I have a right to sell the navigation program. I didn't write it. I don't even understand it, and Rick's attempts to explain do not help. But Rick is my husband. What is mine is his and what is his is mine. That makes it mine to sell." That caused such a stir among the gathered aliens that Max was distracted. Tentacles undulated, feet shifted, mutters filled the room. On his bench up front, Rick uncurled a couple of his larger tentacles. Max had hit a nerve.

Max had more points to make; however, by the time he thought about making them, the judge's platform had revolved, and he was no longer facing Max. With a sigh, Max sat back down. *Damn it.*

No one else stood to speak, and the judge rotated nearly all the way around until he faced Max's family. Then Rick stood. He was short, his walking tentacle curled more than it had been at any time since the pirate invasion.

"I hired Max believing he was moron species and would make a sufficient carrier of young." His tentacles curled more, either because he felt guilty or because he knew how the rest of the universe judged his reproductive methods. Either way, Max wished he was standing down there, his arm tangled with some of those curly fry tentacles.

"He said he was warrior, and I believed he lacked an understanding of the meaning of the word. When I was a moron, I allowed Hunters on my ship. They tried to kill offspring, and Max killed many of them. He had no weapon so he used a maintenance hook to rip out internal organs. Then I knew he was warrior. I offered to return him to a place of safety, and he said he found me desirable. I find him desirable. We name each other husband. He can spend my money. He can claim my work."

That caused even more tentacle twitching, and this time the mutters intensified to chatter, and when half the aliens sounded like cats in heat or tone-deaf opera singers, it made for a pretty cacophonous courtroom.

The judge stood, and Max expected the room to go silent. Instead the room transformed in the blink of an eye into a cocktail party sans drinks. Carrington stood talking to two Chosen ones while Xena headed for the exit. A small crowd had gathered around Bundy, and since he was short, he vanished under the moving wall of tentacles and backs.

What the fuck was going on? Max touched the screen, willing a barrel shaped alien to move aside so Max could get one last look at his family. At Rick. Despite every instinct that told Rick to hide, he was here. He had spoken up and defended Max the best he could. Max had thought he couldn't love Rick more, but he did.

He pressed his palm against the screen as Rick and Kohei pushed through the crowd and walked up the long aisle. Aliens were wandering out now, and Rick moved faster. Max prayed for each second the video continued, for each moment he could bask in Rick's presence. He was beautiful, flowing past aliens and gliding over a bench to avoid a milling group of gossipers who hadn't moved out of his way. He was strong and so damn smart. He didn't need to have boned leg tentacles or a neck to be perfect.

Max pressed his body against the screen, and a vibration ran through the metal. Half afraid of some security measure, Max stepped back. The wall then slid up like a garage door so the camera image of the hearing was projected on the ceiling. Max could see into the courtroom and see Rick charging at him, tentacles waving and his tool hat flopping as it started to slide backward.

Still too stunned to move, Max was knocked backward onto the bench and tentacles were all over him. All over.

"Hey, kids in the room," Max said. They had agreed that naughty touching would not happen in front of the children, and Rick was violating that in spectacular fashion. For a second, Rick froze. The tip of a tentacle pressed against Max's hole, and most of Rick's tentacles were under Max's clothing. With a breathy raspberry that came very close to a sigh, Rick withdrew most of his tentacles. He did leave one under Max's shirt curled around his nipple and a few around Max's waist, but that was almost not inappropriate.

Kohei blew raspberries and stood where Max's cell joined the courtroom. "What happened? Did we win?" Max asked.

Rick bellowed. "Query. Win what?" There were so many things Max wanted to win. His freedom would be high on the list, as would a guarantee that his family would keep their ship.

Kohei answered before Max could figure out which question to ask first. "Max Father, this was evidentiary hearing. There was no winning. But now the authorities have questions on evidence of husbanding."

All the air went out of Max's lungs and his thoughts scattered. Rick tightened his tentacles, and Max managed a weak, "That wasn't a trial?" Both Kohei and Rick stared at him.

"Query," Max added belatedly.

Kohei blew bubbles.

Rick was a little more sympathetic. "If authorities accuse you of wrong doing, a judgment or liability takes many, many months. On Earth television, trials move slow. They keep going and going and going." Rick and his love of commercials.

"This looked like a courtroom. I thought..." Max closed his eyes.

"Max Father, I am sorries for not explaining," Kohei said now that he had finished laughing at Max. "Rational creatures cannot judge so fast."

"Sentient and rational are not the same." Max noticed that neither of them disagreed with him. "So, did the hearing go our way?"

"Authority believes Max is not moron species. Navigation program is not sold," Rick said. More and more aliens were leaving the courtroom... or evidentiary hearing room.

"Where's Dee?" Max asked.

"Other room. Same hearing." Kohei gestured toward the side Max couldn't see from his current position.

"We should go find her."

Dee hadn't known that Carrington was using her. If the universe was just, Carrington was going to have to pay a fine or at the very least, look like an idiot. Bitch. Max realized both his family members were watching him. Rick was motionless, and Kohei was rotating in confusion. Max stood, or at least he tried to. Rick was heavy. He lifted Rick an inch and then they collapsed back down onto the bunk.

Rick untangled his tentacles.

Max tried to find the words that would allow him to explain why he worried about Dee. From their point of view, it didn't make sense, but he didn't want his family to blame her for any of this mess. "She warned me and tried to get me out before the guards showed up."

"How would leaving Carrington's ship have made improved evidence?" Kohei asked.

Well, shit. Kohei had a valid point. Max was in the middle of a con, so whether the authorities caught him there or later, it didn't matter. Eventually they would have found him outside the ship, with or without Dee's warning. Hiding wouldn't have improved their legal position, but Max had an instinct to run for home. Max stood and tightened his hold on Rick's tentacle. "Let's go see if she is all right."

Rick didn't say anything, but he did start toward the main room. His tentacles didn't even curl much. Most of the aliens had left now. Bundy and his entourage hovered near the exit, but everyone else had gone. The judge came off the table once Max stepped into the main room.

The judge shouted. "We will discuss questions of husbanding." The high-tone cut through Max's head.

"I need to check on Dee," Max said firmly.

"I'm here." Dee came out of the cell that was opposite the exit. A few of the aliens around Bundy turned toward them, but then Bundy left and his entourage followed. Dee walked over, stopping several feet away. "I'm fine."

The judge came striding up the aisle with a rolling gait similar to a human. Funny, but the two-legged walk looked strange after months of watching Rick and the kids glide about on their walking tentacles. The judge trumpeted. "I require clarification." And here the rest of the universe complained about Rick's people being too loud. Pot and kettle. Pot and high-pitched, annoying kettle.

"About husbanding. Right. Okay, ask away." Maybe relief was making Max a little punch-drunk because that was not the way to address a judge, not even an alien one. The Chosen judge pushed his lips forward so that his line of nostrils all opened into teardrop shapes. After a second, the face relaxed again.

"I require clarification of human social structure. Are humans required of groups?"

The business translator made language a lot clearer, but the judge had a stilted, wrong quality to his language, even with the improved translation.

Max answered. "Humans do require some sort of social connections. Sometimes they live in isolation, but usually they will have one person they pair bond with or one family member. People who live completely isolated usually end up odd."

Dee snorted. "They end up insane," she corrected him. "It damages their brains." She tapped the side of her head. Given that Dee had been the one abandoned on the planet, Max had avoided saying that. Dee shook her head. "I should have been able to follow his math on those weapons modifications. I have the same background. But I couldn't. But that's not evidence that Max didn't do the work. We were both working on a translation interface, but Max got ten times farther than I did in the same amount of time. And the longer I was alone, the worse my productivity got."

The judge studied Dee and Max. "Both humans were isolated."

"No," Dee said. She smiled at Max before she gave Rick a fond look. "Max had a husband and children. He is a lucky man."

Max pulled Rick closer. "I am."

"Gregariousness can include species not human?" the judge asked. "Odd."

"Humans are odd," Kohei oh-so-helpfully added. The judge ignored him.

"Why did you not seek gregarious group?" the judge asked Dee.

"Because no one would talk to me," she said. "I tried to get to know a few of the people who lived in the same area, but they ignored me."

Max remembered how much it had hurt when he had thought Rick's friendship wasn't real. The sense of loss and the loneliness had nearly eaten him alive. A day of that had nearly broken him. She'd been alone the whole time. "God, Dee, I'm so sorry."

She shrugged. "It's not like you abandoned me. Hell, I walked away from you to take the job with Carrington because I believed all that shit about Hidden ones being parasites. The last I checked, parasites don't risk coming to court to defend their families. Rick, I'm sorry I listened to these assholes."

Rick loosened his hold of Max's arm enough to rotate.

Dee continued while Rick was still rotating back and forth. "I should turn in my POC card. I mean, I know what it's like to have people judge me because of the color of my skin, and I go making assumptions about other people because of where they have their eyes. I am a horrible human being."

Max hated the disgust he heard in her voice. She was a damn good pilot and a good person. Some of the guys from the unit—Max wouldn't want to spend time with them. But Dee was kind and quiet and she would laugh with people without laughing at them. "I probably would have believed what people told me if the translator had worked well enough for my social worker to say anything other than Rick's people were loud and unpopular," Max told her. But he didn't want to go further into the topic of discrimination in front of a judge. This might not have been a trial, but important rulings still had to get made.

He turned to the judge. "Can I sell the navigation program or not?" Maybe his con had backfired a bit, but he still wanted to make enough profit to get upgrades for the ship. He was going to have to do a lot of security audits and new weapon designs to get the credits they needed if he couldn't sell Rick's programming.

They could go back to Hidden planet and sell it under the official terms of the sanction agreement, but Max was vindictive enough that he didn't want these people to get access to the technology unless they were willing to pay a fair price. Cutting off one's nose to spite one's face was a valid hobby on Earth, one that Max endorsed.

"We must discuss husbanding with Ugly one." The judge turned and walked back toward the table in the center of the room. Asshole. Kohei followed the judge, and Rick tugged at Max to do the same. Maybe the evidentiary hearing wasn't over. Max took a deep breath. If his ability to make a living depended on the alien understanding of husbanding, he knew one thing. He wouldn't deny Rick. Maybe they had never stood in front of an altar in a church, but in Max's heart, they were married. Nothing would change that.

And if this asshole called Rick ugly again, Max would take it out on the judge's legs, and since he had kneecaps, Max knew exactly where to kick him.

Chapter Twenty-One

The judge got up onto his table again, but this time it didn't rotate. He considered the small group of them. Dee stood slightly to one side, but Kohei was so close that Max could only tell the tentacle tips apart because Kohei's had far more beige and green and Rick had more red.

"What definition do you give for husbanding?" the judge asked.

Max smiled at Rick. "Mating. Pair bonding. Sharing sameness for the rest of our lives."

Rick's tentacles shivered.

"How many individuals are inside husbanding?"

"As the only female here," Dee said, "I should point out that marriage doesn't always involve husbands. You're leaving out wives."

The judge turned toward her. "Define wife."

"The female equivalent of husband," Dee said. "A wife is a female who is in a marriage. A husband is a male who is in a marriage."

"Define female," the judge said. Dee opened her mouth, but Max quickly jumped in.

"Careful," Max warned. "That word will lead you down a rabbit trail, and somewhere along the way, you're going to decide that you don't know what female means, and I say this as a male who carried and gave birth to three children."

She grimaced. "Yikes. You have a point." She turned to the judge. "But I can say that I call myself a female, so I am one. If I join a marriage, then I would be a wife, not a husband."

The judge tapped something on his wrist translator. "How many individuals are inside marriaging?"

"Two," Max said. Yeah, there were polygamists, but that was another rabbit trail he was not going down.

"Define length and termination of marriaging."

Max wanted to say that marriage was forever, but being in the military meant he had seen entirely too many marriages fail. Trying to maintain a relationship when one partner kept getting deployed wasn't easy. "Most humans hope that marriage will last forever, but honestly, sometimes it doesn't. Sometimes people change and after a time, they find that they don't fit together anymore. Then they get a divorce."

The judge tapped on his wrist translator again. "Is 'fit' a reference to tentacles and intestines?" he asked.

Dee snorted.

"No!" Max blurted. Oh god. Obviously the rest of the universe knew how Hidden ones reproduced, but that was not a topic he ever wanted to discuss. Nope. He might enjoy tentacle sex, but he did not enjoy talking about it. "No, it's more about having compatible goals. Sometimes people decide they want different things."

"And sometimes," Dee added, "people live together for their entire lives. They raise children and grandchildren. They love each other until the end of their lives, and when one dies, the other never recovers and they live a half-life."

That was specific.

"My grandparents," she added.

"My parents have been married for forty years. That will probably be them." Max focused on the judge again. "That's the goal of most humans—to have a marriage that will last forever." Max tightened his hold on Rick's tentacle. Maybe Rick understood the gesture because he leaned closer and wrapped a tentacle around Max's arm. God, Max didn't even know how long Hidden ones lived. He selfishly hoped it was a very long time. He couldn't bear the pain of losing Rick, not even if that meant Rick had to lose him.

Completely oblivious to the emotional moment, the judge had the gall to continue the official hearing. "The translation matrix translates marriaging to a non-economic term. Clarify the economics of marriaging."

"What's mine is yours and what's yours is mine, for better and for worse, in sickness and in health," Max said. "Those are some of the vows we take when we marry."

More tapping on the translator. Max had the feeling that he was being asked to create a legal definition—one that all humans would have to live up to. These people made judgments—like humans were morons—and then they blithely assumed every conclusion they reached was right. As far as Max was concerned, that made them morons. The judge looked up. "Clarify, time of vows between you and Ugly one."

"Okay, no!" Max held up a finger of warning, which was the same gesture his mother had used every time Max had traipsed mud over her floors. "You do not get to insult him by calling him ugly."

The judge raised his head on that awkwardly long neck. "Ugly one is official designation, not insult."

"Well it's pretty fucking insulting."

Rick blurbled a quiet, "Max," but Max ignored that.

"They are called the Hidden ones. If my people get up here... No, when they get up here because they will work together and get their asses into space now that they know the rest of the universe is flying over their heads. So, when they get here, they might choose to call you Big Nostril aliens or Freaky Lip aliens or even Ugly ones." The judge's nostrils all tightened to slits. "But they will at least call you that in private. They won't walk up to your face and say it."

"Preach it," Dee said quietly.

The judge stared at Max for a long time before he glanced at Rick and Kohei, who was pressed close to his father's side. Then he looked back at Max. "Official hearing requires official nomenclature," the judge said. "I shall designate the Ugly one 'Rick' to avoid insulting. Clarify time of vows between you and Rick."

Since Max was not going to win the fight over what the universe called Rick's species, he focused on the question. "To have vows, we needed witnesses, so we never officially had vows."

"Clarify the not using small Ugly on—"

"Ah!" Max held up a finger and spoke loud enough to stop the judge from finishing his thought. "Those are my children. If you call them ugly, I will be unreasonable."

Rick tightened his hold over Max's arm. That was a fairly strong suggestion that Max was on the edge of the local version of a contempt of court charge, but he was not going to let this guy insult his kids.

"I am ignorant of the designations for the small—" The judge thrust his lips out without finishing his sentence. Max still knew exactly what he was thinking.

"This is Kohei," Max said before the judge could say something that Max would not forgive. "Back at the ship, James and Xander are waiting for us to return."

The judge drew his lips back in. "Clarify the not using Kohei, James and Xander as witnesses for official vows."

"They were short one judge for a wedding," Dee said.

The judge turned toward Dee. "Clarify function of judge."

Max took that one. "A judge is an official of public or government organizations."

"Or you could have a minister marry you," Dee added. "But without a judge or a minister, a marriage isn't legal. And before you ask, a minister is an official of the church, which is a system of beliefs."

The judge swiveled his head from Max to Dee and back again .He leaned back on his table. "Clarify. Humans have officials of beliefs. Affirmative or negative?"

Since the judge was turned toward Max, he answered. "We do. I mean, humans in general do. My family isn't terribly religious, but religion is pretty common." Max closed his mouth when the judge's head tilted. He had no idea what that gesture meant, but he knew that people took religion seriously, and the judge's whole species once believed they were chosen by God. So silence was the best strategy here.

"Designated Rick, do you recognize the validity of Unbalanced one's marriage?"

Max blinked. Unbalanced? Max hoped they were talking about human walking and not psychology. He also suspected that hope was in vain. Rick had warned him that he was making himself look like a psycho.

"I do," Rick said. "I am husband to Max and he is husband to me."

"Husbanding can be terminated. Then Rick has circumscribed laws regulating sale of—" The judge stopped. No doubt he was wondering how unbalanced Max might get if he said ugly again. If these guys ever picked up American television broadcasts and saw old episodes of Dexter or pretty much any true crime documentary, they were going to shoot down human ships the second they appeared in the more populated parts of space.

"I would not terminate husbanding!" Rick sounded offended down to his last curling tentacle. When they left the hearing and lost access to the business translator, Max was going to miss being able to hear Rick's emotions reflected in his tone.

"You legally have the right to terminate husbanding. Even Unbalanced Max says as much. This is unacceptable. Unbalanced Max has committed unacceptable trading."

That did not sound good.

Rick blasted a whale-song that didn't translate. "I take Max as..." The statement ended in a belch-song.

"That didn't translate," Max said.

Rick didn't explain—the judge did. "Some species not asymmetrical create relationship that cannot be terminated. What belongs to one belongs to the other. Asymmetrical species do not register such relationships."

"I am husband to Max. I register..." And that was another belch-song.

The judge turned to Max. "Do Unbalanced ones have a marriage relationship that cannot be ended?"

"Um, yeah." Unfortunately, the business translator was going to broadcast his uncertainty. One of the guys in the unit had been Mormon, and he had expected his marriage to survive death and didn't believe divorce was possible because their souls had been joined in a temple. However, that was not part of Max's more nebulous religious tradition. "Churches have that."

"So do laws," Dee said. "My cousin has a covenant marriage registered with the state of Louisiana. That comes with a lot more rules, and it's designed to remain 'til-death-do-us-part very literally. So... " She shrugged.

Rick straightened his tentacles. "I register a covenant marriage." He was using the same belch-song, but the computer had obviously accepted Dee's translation. "He may have access to my possessions. He may buy or sell from my account."

"And you can buy or sell from mine," Max said. "In fact, most people who get married only have one account and both people have access to it."

"Logical," the judge said. "A covenant marriage cannot be voided. If you no longer fit or are not having compatible goals, each will still have access to the account of the other."

Max took a deep breath. "I am fine with that."

Rick grabbed Max with several tentacles. "I am happy with that," he said. And with the fancy translator running, joy filled his voice.

"Describe Unbalanced ones' requirement for vows and I will register marriaging and covenant marriage."

"Um, we say vows to each other in front of witnesses and then file paperwork so the government knows that we are married." Max looked at Dee to see if she had anything to add. She nodded without saying anything. He could add that family should be present, but he was nervous enough about having Kohei and Rick off the ship. He couldn't have all the kids vulnerable at once, and they sure as hell couldn't leave the ship undefended.

"I am ignorant of the vow to say," Rick said.

Max had watched enough television to have a general idea of what he should say, but he didn't think standard words described their rather non-standard relationship. "You say what you feel. Traditionally, you say I promise to love and respect you, in sickness and in health, for better or for worse, for the rest of our lives. But I would add that I will always love the way you blow raspberries when I say something stupid and never hold the stupidity against me. I love that you're patient and I promise to try to avoid trying your patience too much. I love what a good father you are, and I promise to always work with you to raise beautiful children. No matter what the universe throws at us, I promise that I will always put you first because you are my family."

Rick rotated a little, but he couldn't go far without loosening some of his tentacles, and he didn't do that. Then Rick spoke, his translated voice soft with emotion. "I promise to love and respect you, in sickness and in health, for better or for worse, for the rest of our lives. I would add that I will always love the way you tangle tentacles with me when I am afraid or angry and you never tell me to stop having fear or anger. I love that you're caring and I promise to try to avoid..." Rick hesitated. "What should I avoid?" he asked.

Max laughed. "You don't have to avoid anything because you are perfect."

Rick blew raspberries. "I promise to avoid noticing that you do not see me clearly. I love what a good father you are, and I promise to only trust you with our beautiful children. No matter what the universe throws at us, I promise that I will always put you first because you are my family."

"Now you kiss," Dee said.

Considering where Rick's mouth was, that might have been awkward, but Rick brought his largest arm tentacle up and brushed it across Max's mouth. Max caught it and kissed the red tip.

"Woo hoo!" Dee clapped and whistled.

Rick's tentacles spasmed, pulling Max off balance. "Explain noise!" he bellowed while Max tried to get his feet under him without stepping on any tentacle tips. Luckily, Rick was strong enough to hold him while he did it.

"Making noise is traditional to congratulate the new couple," Dee said. "This is me congratulating you and making noise to let everyone know that I wish you many years of happy married life."

Rick's tentacles relaxed, which made it much easier for Max to right himself, and Kohei started bellowing. After a second, the judge added his whistlish cries. Max pulled his shirt down. "Next time, warn Rick before you do that."

"I thought he was sweeping you off your feet," Dee said with a smile. "Congratulations. Both of you."

The judge tapped his wrist translator. "Traditional congratulations. I recorded the covenant marriage. Unbalanced Max is allowed to sell the work of Ugly Rick."

Before Max could say anything, the judge retreated to the far side of the table. Since he had been recording an official document, he probably needed to use the official titles, so Max decided to be charitable and forgo any knee-cracking. Besides, this was his wedding day.

"We should have pictures," Max said. "After I get out of these clothes." They were still dirty from the weapons testing he had been doing with Xena.

"I will speak to Unbalanced Dee of damage from lack of gregariousness." The judge backed toward the far door.

"What about it?" Dee asked.

"We speak elsewhere." The judge continued to back away.

After rolling her eyes, Dee followed. "I'll see you guys later. Don't take off." She stopped and gave Max a searching look.

"Never leave anyone behind," he said.

She smiled and gave him a quick nod before she turned and followed the judge toward the far door.

"What is traditional after a marriage?" Kohei asked.

Max blinked. No way in hell was he explaining the concept of honeymoon to his children. Nope. Let them figure out what parents did the same way all the Earth kids did—by watching television. It might not be the most accurate depiction of adult relationships, but the longer Max had kids, the more he understood why parents did not discuss some things. Kids had a bad habit of asking awkward questions.

"We should find food Max likes. He picks at ship food without enjoying," Rick said.

"You noticed?"

Rick blew raspberries. "We will sell the navigation program to the one you designate Al Bundy and then we will find you food you enjoy. I dislike watching you put food in your mouth the way a—whale song-eats a—burb—"

Feeling almost nostalgic, Max said, "Translation matrix failure."

Rick tightened his hold.

Husbands. They were actual husbands. Odd husbands, but Max had grown used to odd. He even kinda liked it. Max squeezed his husband's tentacle.

Chapter Twenty-Two

"Rick Father, Max Father!" Xander flew at them the second the ship door opened. The unemotional translation computer didn't communicate excitement, but Xander's volume and speed did.

"Xander!" Max gave him a hug, and when James followed, Max bent over to pull him in close. It took Rick a couple of seconds, then he was there, curling his tentacles around the younger two kids, and finally Kohei joined in. Max had tentacles everywhere, and he assumed the one down the back of his pants was Rick's.

"I'm so glad you guys are safe." Standing safely in their ship with his whole family around him, the cold fear that had wrapped around Max's heart eased.

James twitched all of his tentacles. "We are much with safety. We were always much with safety. You and Rick Father were not with safety. We worried."

"Sorry, buddy." Max hugged James tighter for a second before standing.

"Max Father," Xander said, "Al Bundy sent a message. He says he can sell Rick Father's navigation program. He says people pay almost as much as when Rick Father was unknown."

"Hey, that's great." Not as great as getting full price, but "almost" was going to have to be enough. He could only ask the universe to improve so much because the prejudices against the Hidden ones went deep. Max wondered how much of the prejudice was the whole asymmetrical issue and how much came from the aggravation the rest of the universe felt at having navigation in that part of space shut down.

Rick's people weren't warriors. From what Max had seen on the videos, they still considered hunting a skill every Hidden one should possess. They hunted the small prey on their planet. But the idea of fighting something nearly the same size or fighting another sentient creature didn't exist for them. And the rest of the universe could not respect that a species whose only survival strategy was hiding might not want warriors running around their part of space. Max could testify that when aliens ran past your planet, sometimes it did not end well.

"Do you hear that?" Max asked Rick. "You are going to get credit for writing that program."

"My hearing is unimpaired to hear Xander's words."

Apparently Max's enthusiasm had been lost under the literal translation of his words. Max was going to miss that business translation program.

"Max Father," Xander said, "The official translation program now translates human as Unbalanced one."

Max grimaced. "Is that a reference to human walking or human thinking?"

"The translation of the word unbalanced implies both."

Rick blew bubbles.

Max rolled his eyes. "Yeah, yeah, yeah. Is that you saying I told you so?"

When Rick stared at him, Max realized that Rick hadn't understood the question. "Query," he started. "Are you implying that I should have listened to you when you warned me that I was making myself sound violent?"

Rick bugled. "Yes."

Max pulled Rick closer. "Well, at least the rest of the universe has fair warning that they need to leave my husband and my children alone. I can be unreasonable when people threaten them, even if the threats are only economic."

"Is more," Xander said, his tentacles flailing. "Translation of Ugly one has asterisk."

Max assumed that wasn't a literal asterisk, but that someone had flagged the translation in some way. "What does that mean?"

"Unknown." Xander rotated a bit. "Perhaps they warn not to use designation Ugly one near Max Father."

"That would be wise. I will admit that I feel a little homicidal every time I hear someone say that." Max wasn't sure how long he could control his urge to punch someone. In ROTC, they had made a big deal out of service members being unofficial ambassadors. They had to represent America well to the rest of the world. However, those instructors never had to put up with fucking aliens.

"Max generates unstable words." Rick didn't pull away, so he wasn't too worried about Max's version of unbalanced.

"Will you protested the designation of human as unbalanced?" James asked. He had a weird bounce in his tentacles that made Max worry that James wanted a fight. Given his namesake, he might turn out to be the only Hidden one who wanted conflict.

"I probably should. The rest of the humans probably won't be amused." Max walked deeper into the ship. The door slid closed automatically when the family followed. Kohei hurried ahead to trigger the elevator. "But on the good side, if humans have a reputation for being unbalanced, the rest of the universe is less likely to poke us with a sharp stick."

"Sharp stick is unprobable," Rick said. "Sharp maintenance hook more probable."

Max laughed. "Metaphorically, the universe has a lot of sharp sticks lying around—insults, unjust sanctions, maintenance hooks." Max's stomach rumbled. "Come on, let's get something to eat. There should have been a delivery of new foods."

"Many, many," James offered. "Available by computer."

Max might get a decent meal. It had been so long that he wasn't sure what good food tasted like anymore, but he had found several things at the market that he had liked, at least when sampling them. "We should talk about what we're going to do with all of those new credits we're going to have from Rick Father's program."

"And credits from weapons Max Father and I sell," James added with a furious little wave of his tentacles.

Max gave the closest waving tentacle a gentle tug. "Of course. We can't forget that."

"No." Rick bugled. "You must reserve credits of yours. When you are ready to be James On Your Own, you must have reserve. Reserve James will not be spent on ship of Max and Rick." He bugled again. Rick had a good point, even if Max sometimes liked to pretend that the children would be with them forever.

James had his tentacles drawn up, which usually meant a family fight was about two seconds away. "My credits. I am spending on my wanting."

"How about we have a compromise, kiddo," Max interrupted. "When I was young, my parents had me put half my money into a savings account for the future. The other half I could spend if I was buying something reasonable."

James's tentacles uncurled, but Rick's tentacles drew up. Max leaned in closer. "Trust me," he whispered to Rick. Rick did a quarter turn and considered him out of several small eyes. Max suspected that indicated something like disbelief or sarcasm. He wondered if each of the eyes represented a different emotion. However, Max was not going to explain in front of James that they could simply put money aside for each of the kids and then make them take it since it was a human tradition for parents to economically support their children. None of the kids were going to be left without resources to do whatever they wanted to do in life.

They left the elevator and were headed toward the only room large enough for all of them to eat together—the pool room. They were almost there when Rick stopped. Max frowned, watching as Rick read something on his wrist translator.

"Human Dee requests entrance to the ship." Rick studied Max with his largest eye.

"Do you have a problem with her?" Max asked.

"No."

"Then let's go let her in." Max reversed course and headed back into the elevator. Having Dee around was potential trouble. After all, if Rick's ship... if their ship... had been close enough to pick up television and the kids were sure to tell her, then they could have gone home.

But no matter how much potential trouble Max could be in, he wouldn't leave her behind. You didn't do that to your unit. He touched the release on the outer door. Outside on the ramp stood Dee with a large bag sitting at her feet.

"Hey, how are you?"

"Good," Dee said. "Permission to come on board?"

"Come on in." Max stepped to one side. "What happened with the judge?" Max led her toward the elevator, leaving the door to close automatically.

"It turns out, I had quite the basis for a lawsuit because their government's stupidity left me lacking a basic necessity for human life." Dee hiked her bag up higher on her shoulder.

"Companionship."

"Yep. I got a financial settlement to make up for the government's stupidity. Apparently they have decided I am not from a moronic species as much as from an emotionally fragile one, and I couldn't argue the point."

They got into the elevator, and Max tried to figure out a way to apologize. He hadn't thought to ask if any other humans had survived.

And they had ignored so many of his requests that he had stopped asking for anything. "I'm so sorry."

"No worries. To compensate me for my significant trauma," and her tone made it clear she was quoting the judge on that one, "they gave me a shit-ton of money. So I tried to hire a ship to take me back to Earth," Dee said in a cheerful voice as she stepped off the elevator.

"And? Did you find one?" Max knew she had a husband of her own back on Earth. No doubt, he assumed she was dead. Max prayed that didn't end in some disaster for poor Dee. She'd suffered enough without going home to find her husband married to someone else. God, those months he'd spent watching television with the kids while Rick worked on his program had rotted his brain. He thought in soap opera plots now. He didn't mind pop culture dominating most of his brain, but he could not conduct threat assessments using soap opera plots.

"When Earth was a back-water Hicksville, getting a ticket would have been impossibly expensive."

"Yeah, I remember." That had been the main reason Max had taken the nanny job, not that he was complaining. That job had turned out damn well.

"You have the world's stupidest love-sick grin right now."

"The universe's stupidest," Max corrected her.

"At the very least, the galaxy's," she conceded. "However, it turns out that now no one wants to fly to the planet of the Unbalanced ones." She gave him a weary look. "I know you did ROTC instead of OTS, but did anyone ever mention the part where you're supposed to be a role model for the people you encounter?"

Max sniffed and shrugged one-shoulder style. "They mentioned something about ambassadors, but in my defense, they told me I had to represent Americans well, not Earthlings."

Dee shook her head, her amusement evident.

"I take it you need a ride back to Earth." Most of the good-will evaporated from Max's heart. He had to go home—he had parents and a little brother back there in the chaos. But going back to Earth meant handling the prejudices of his own people. That was not Max's happy thought for the day.

"It would be nice. Is Rick going that way?"

"Um, maybe. We can ask him."

And Rick would say absolutely, and Max would have to figure out something to say to the Air Force. Well, he had to face his home world eventually. Max opened the door to the pool room. The computer interface table had been joined by a lower and larger table the family would use for shared meals, and that was where they were all waiting. Everyone except Rick. He was close to the door. When Max came in, Rick curled a tentacle around his wrist.

"Hey, everyone. You remember Dee. It turns out that I've scared everyone away from Earth and no one will give her a ride back home, not even with all the money the government gave her to apologize for their general shittiness."

"Which was a lot, but that's fair because it was a lot of shittiness," Dee said with a smile. "It's nice to see you folks again." She smiled at Rick and then at the kids. They all watched, silent.

Max pulled Rick closer. "So, what do you say we give Dee a ride back to Earth?" After the fact, Max added, "Query."

Rick's tentacles curled. "Change of attitude toward Hidden ones is alarm for Hidden ones on Hidden planet. Change is unfathomable without unknown data."

"Query. Do you want to go to Hidden planet and explain the changes to your people?" Max asked. He wouldn't mind that... not a little. It would give him more time to figure out what he might say to his commanders... and his parents. He didn't know how to introduce Richard and Velma Davis to their alien grandchildren.

"Hidden ones and unknown are not two great tastes that taste great together." Rick's tentacles were curling tighter by the second.

Dee gave Rick an odd look. Yep, that had pretty much outed them as having contact with Earth. However, Dee didn't address that. "Hey, I thought I was going to die of old age out here, so if you can get me home to my family any time before never, that's a good deal. I can wait."

"Clarify deal. I require not compensation from Dee Friend of Max Husband. No deal." That made some of his tentacles straighten back out.

"Dee uses the word deal in non-standard way to suggest gratitude," Max said. "She is not suggesting compensation."

"Nope, but I did bring a gift." Dee put her bag onto the floor and dug around. When she stood, she had a box that made Rick's tentacles go so straight that he gained several inches of height. Xander made a low bellow and Kohei started waving his tentacles. James actually dropped his food onto the table, where it rolled off and the slope of the floor sent it heading toward the water.

"Since a wedding gift is traditional and I can't spend my settlement on a ticket home, I thought I would buy you guys a business translator." She smiled as she held out the suitcase-sized object.

"Best present ever!" Xander shouted. Max couldn't have agreed more.

Chapter Twenty-Three

As soon as the door to their private quarters closed, Max let out his breath. God, this had been the longest day ever, or at least the longest day in the last couple of months. However, now they were alone and they had the fancy new translator installed into the main computer. Dee knew how to gift right. He turned and looked at Rick. "Whatever will we do now?" Max asked in a teasing voice as he pulled his shirt off. He even threw in an eyebrow wiggle.

Rick rotated a few degrees. "We could do—" Rick's suggestion ended in whale song. Having an improved translator didn't mean perfect communication, and Rick didn't get eyebrow semaphore.

"That didn't translate. Can you describe what you mean?"

Rick began the explanation with whale song. "—is touching where partners pull on each other's tentacles and attempt to cause pleasure until sexual orifices open."

That sounded vaguely unhygienic. "Open? Query. Clarify open."

"Similar to when you ejaculate and the hole the sperm and lubrication comes out of opens," Rick explained in the universe's least sexy description of sex. However, if there was an activity that would give Rick enough pleasure to make a sexual orifice open, Max was in favor of it. He unbuttoned his pants rather than risk another Rick-disaster with clothing. There was a small possibility that Rick's people didn't wear clothes because they couldn't keep up with the mending.

"I'm down for it. And maybe after I do this, we can figure out a name for it. So, how do we start?"

That got a full quarter turn out of Rick. "You start pulling tentacles by pulling tentacles." Max would have expected that to come with a "duh" tone, but the new translator made Rick sound cautious... timid.

Max sat on the edge of their bed and held a hand out. Rick slid closer, his center tentacle undulating. "Is there a particular tentacle I should pull or a way that I can do it to make you feel more pleasure?"

"All pulling is pleasurable with you." Rick probably meant that as a factual reassurance, but that had to be the sweetest thing Max had ever heard. The casual way that he said it was the cherry on the sundae.

"Spending any time together is pleasurable with you." Max caught a red-tipped tentacle and gently pulled. When he didn't get a reaction, he pulled a little harder. Rick wasn't fragile. Hell, he was stronger than Max, but Max still hesitated. "Could I hurt you doing this?"

"Unlikely." Rick paused, and his tentacles got a little curlier. "Query. Could I hurt you by pulling on your tentacles?"

Max doubted that Rick would ever get rough enough to do harm, but he also didn't want to encourage any carelessness. "If you pull too hard, you could damage my joints."

Rick trumpeted and yanked most of his tentacles away. Max held onto the one he had been trying to pull. "That is why unboned tentacles are more practical than boned ones. Had I known I could create damage, I would have worried about ways I have pulled your tentacles in a past." The translator let all the concern and horror come shining through. It was sweet. However, the concern was overkill.

"I enjoy the way you pull my tentacle."

Rick noticed that he had switched to a singular noun. "Query. You reference your one logical tentacle."

Max laughed. Rick had commented on the lack of bones in Max's dick more than once. "Yes, I am. You are very good at pulling that tentacle, and you have always been careful to avoid damage. If you have never broken my dick, you're not going to damage my arm."

Rick's tentacles didn't relax. "If we are pulling tentacles and not seeking genetic release, I anticipate pulling more. Query. Would more pulling damage your logical tentacle?"

"Well, maybe take it easy pulling my cock," Max admitted. As strong as Rick was, if he applied force to Max's cock, that was not going to end well. "It is a fairly fragile tentacle. My arms and legs are tougher, even with the joints. So, back to my original question, how hard can I pull on your tentacles before damaging them? I am uncomfortable doing something which could cause harm." Max ran his fingers along the underside of the tentacle he was holding captive.

"I will tell you if the unlikely chance the pulling is too much. You will not hurt me." Rick curled a red tentacle tip around Max's wrist. Max started pulling, gently at first. When he didn't get a reaction, he pulled harder, and harder. Rick shivered.

"Good?"

"Exceptionally. It is more good because it is you that pulls." Rick brought a few more tentacles around to curl around Max's arms.

"You are a sweet talker."

Rick blew raspberries. "I believe that translated incorrectly. My talent does not include talent with speech."

"Really?" Max put a little more muscle into tugging, and Rick shivered so hard that his tentacles came loose, falling off Max's arms. "I would say you are very talented with speech." Max waited until Rick recovered and brought a few of his tentacles back up before pulling as if he was in boot camp and his drill sergeant was watching. Rick grunted and shimmied.

"Too much?" Max let go of the tentacle.

"No. You pull wonderfully. I didn't expect such goodness with pulling," Rick said.

"I need you to talk to me and tell me you're okay," Max said.

Rick blew a raspberry. "I have no ability to think logical thoughts when you pull my tentacles."

"Then I am going to pull your tentacles more often. However, I need some reassurance that what I'm doing is good, and you don't need to be logical."

"You should demonstrate." Rick pounced on Max, curling tentacles around his arms and pushing Max back onto the bed. Before Max could formulate a plan to counter-attack, Rick tugged on Max's arm. For a half second, Max was eye to enormous eye with Rick, and then Rick braced other tentacles on Max's torso and pushed.

"Oh yeah." Max's shoulder popped and muscles stretched. "Fuck yeah. More."

Rick pushed until Max was turned partially on his side, a tentacle braced against his ass. Max wiggled, and Rick pulled on his leg and arm at the same time. Max arched his back and groaned.

"Is that positive or negative feedback?" Rick asked as he eased the pressure.

"Positive. I think you popped my back, and that feels glorious." Max used Rick's temporary distraction to counter-attack, tugging the tentacle that was wrapped around his wrist. Max put his back into it and strained. Rick shimmied with pleasure, releasing his hold over Max. Then several of his tentacles stiffened before turning to jelly. Max had found the sweet spot. He jerked the tentacle again, and Rick made an unfamiliar gargle-grunt. "Do you like that?"

"Fuck yeah, positive feedback. More." Rick echoed Max's earlier words. Awww. Max had taught his sweet little octopus to swear.

Max reached for a shorter tentacle. The minute he caught it, the red tip curled around his wrist and Rick shivered. "Tell me if I am close to hurting you."

"I do not have illogical joinings of bones to make weakness."

Max experimented by jiggling the tentacle he was holding. "How does that feel?"

"Jerky movements are more odd than pleasurable," Rick said. And he sounded much more coherent, which meant Max was going in the wrong direction. He wanted to drive Rick to the point that he couldn't form rational thoughts. He pulled the tentacle, but Rick countered with a sneak attack. The tentacle under Max's back caught Max's wrist and yanked it. Max lost his hold on the tentacle he'd captured.

Rick pushed Max's hip away while tugging his arm closer. It meant Max was twisted oddly on the bed, but his back was getting the best stretch ever. "Fuck yeah," he said with a groan. Tensions that had set into his bones leaked out every pore. "Do the other side," he begged.

Rick crawled over Max, his weight leaving Max breathless for a second before he slid over to the other side. Then Rick repeated the push-pull-twist maneuver on the other side. Max's spine crackled and he groaned in pleasure. Knots he'd had since college all melted away. "Hell yes." Max grunted when Rick curled a tentacle around his thigh. With the walking tentacle firmly in the small of Max's back, Rick stretched Max's right arm and leg, making his spine crack.

Max turned his body over to Rick's care. "Oh fuck yeah." He sighed the words as his muscles yielded. Shivers travelled up his spine and Max's eyes fell closed as Rick manipulated him. Time slid past as Rick rolled him around the bed, and Max was too blissed-out to care. When Rick finished stretching Max's last finger, Rick settled on top of Max, resting against Max's sweaty shoulder. Max had no idea why he was sweating because Rick had done most of the work. However, he was too relaxed and comfortable to care.

"Did you enjoy—?" more whale song.

Max thought about it for a second. He considered massage, but there was more muscle work involved, and he had stretched in ways that didn't match that idea. He said, "Sexy yoga. That was very, very sexy yoga." Max groaned as he tried to shift his ass over an inch. His muscles protested that he was too loose and relaxed to move.

"Did you enjoy sexy yoga?"

"I loved it," Max said. He had never enjoyed intimacy without his dick getting involved, and he had been missing out. "Did you enjoy it?"

Max felt a niggle of worry that he had not been very good at pulling tentacles. He was more the pullee.

"It's grrrrreat!" Rick trumpeted in a good imitation of a cartoon tiger. He was watching too much television, and coming from Max, that was saying something. Rick stroked Max's side, his tentacles warm against Max's skin. "Humans and Hidden ones are exceptionally compatible." Rick settled in against Max . He was an island of heat as the rest of Max's body cooled.

"You and I are compatible, that's for sure. But I feel guilty because I gave up pulling on your tentacles somewhere in the middle."

"That always happens," Rick said. "I don't often win, but I like to win."

Max pried one eye open. "Win? What did you win?"

"I won the—" whale song.

"You won? I didn't know it was a competition."

Rick trumpeted. "You tried to win."

"I did not."

"Did too."

Max smiled and curled his arm around the closest bunch of tentacles.

Rick slid tentacles down Max's body and between his legs, but Max was too damn relaxed to get hard. He had never thought that was possible, especially not when he was in bed with Rick. He had a real thing for his minty-green octopus. "So," Max paused to kiss the tentacle that teased his lips. "What was I trying to win?"

"You hoped to pull my muscles until I was too full of pleasure to move."

Max chuckled. "True enough. And instead, you did that to me."

"Point!" Rick said, his voice full of joy. "I won. I almost never win. And I did not realize humans were competitive in same way as Hidden ones were competitive."

"You can win with me any time," Max said. "But right now, I am too tired to talk." He let his eyes drift closed again. He had never been so relaxed in his whole life.

"Because you are compatible with Hidden ones. I am sorry you do not have a place for putting genetic material, but I enjoyed producing inseminating fluids." And that was a smug voice.

"You... haven't you come in the past?" Max asked. That disturbed him.

Rick blew raspberries against Max's shoulder. "We played at egg implantation. Egg implantation does not produce inseminating fluids. I enjoy greatly egg implantation, but I also enjoy greatly pulling tentacles, and being the one to produce inseminating fluids was unanticipated joy. I enjoy all roles of sexual reproduction with you, even when we are not reproducing."

"Me too." Max rolled onto his side and threw an arm around Rick's torso. "Definitely."

They lay as the lights automatically dimmed because of their inactivity. Max was almost asleep when Rick added. "I would also enjoy egg implantation without playing."

Max waited for the shock or the distress at the idea of Rick putting more eggs in him, but that feeling never materialized. "Maybe later." Max wanted to get his first set of kids settled first, and then they had to take Dee home and Max had to deal with Earth after they visited the Hidden world. They already had a full agenda, but the day might come when another egg implantation would be nice. But this moment was for the two of them. He tightened his arms around Rick and sighed when tentacles tightened around him in return. For now, this was all Max needed.

Also by Lyn Gala